# STRAIGHT MEN

## JONATHAN W. THURSTON

Guernsey Memorial Library
3 Court Street
Norwich, NY 13815
www.guernseymemoriallibrary.org

ISBN: 978-1-68433-093-5
PUBLISHED BY BLACK ROSE WRITING
www.blackrosewriting.com

Printed in the United States of America
Suggested Retail Price (SRP) $17.95

*Straight Men* is printed in Chaparral Pro

To those readers who helped bring this book to its greatest potential, including Bill Kieffer, Hypetaph, Tabsley, and Sherayah Witcher, thank you. To the real-life Mason419, whom I had the misfortune of meeting once...fuck you.

# STRAIGHT MEN

# PROLOGUE

Off the main highway, a country road wound through a dense thicket. The slender trunks of birch trees loomed over the frost-covered path, and their shadows stretched across the road, shielding it from the rays of the setting sun. If one followed the path, with that crimson sun always to the right, the road would roll over more birch-covered hills and across a shallow ravine that trickled slowly along to a fishing pond that now was darker than even the road. And if one kept going on the road, one would come past a small cemetery with four unmarked graves, a pasture with two roan horses openly grazing, a decrepit barn with its windows boarded and its door removed, and a fenced-in dirt yard with a two-story house in its center. Outside the fence was a mailbox with the number 419 hastily written on a sticky note Scotch-taped to it, with the name "MASON" in all capital letters printed on white stickers below that. And right past the mailbox stood a large doghouse with a young German shepherd lying halfway in its doorway, the name "Max" painted in black right above the entrance.

While Max slept with the sunset basking his black fur in its red, fading light, his ears flicked when he heard the sound of a high-pitched scream coming from the house. Max turned his head a few inches and moved deeper into the sleep, unconcerned.

The screams persisted, this time, with words attached to them: "Please, sir, don't! I won't do it again, sir. *Please!*"

Past the doghouse and up the walkway to the front door, its windowpanes spiderwebbing with cracks, the house's white paint could be seen visibly peeling with vines curling up the walls and around the storm drain. Through the front door, the house looked much cleaner and well taken care of. The living room had a black leather couch in the back with a small television across from it on a stand. An overhead light attached to a ceiling fan bathed the room in a dim golden glow, and in the room's center, a tall, bearded man in jeans and a loose-fitting t-shirt stood over a much younger man, maybe twenty or so, who was on his knees and entirely naked except for a web of ropes that bound his hands to his feet behind his back. His head was held back by a similar rope that attached to a collar around his neck. Blood oozed from lacerations across the young man's face, arms, and chest, and dripped from the hunting knife in the older man's veined fist. The blood dribbled down onto a black tarp spread across the floor under the two people.

"I promise, sir, I won't do it again!" the younger man pleaded.

The older man's bald head was turning red with his rage. "You shouldn't have disobeyed me in the first place, *slut!*" He swung with a wide arc, slashing the boy across the tip of his nose, causing him to cough and sputter as the blood poured over his lips. The boy screamed again. "You *kissed* him! You fucking *kissed* him! You invited him into *my* house without *my* permission, and you *kissed* him!" He swung again, this time lacerating one of the boy's cheeks.

"*Please, sir!*" the boy begged, tears running down his face and stinging his cheeks, while snot and blood ran over his mouth.

The older man went down on one knee, running his fingers through the boy's hair, pulling it where it met the scalp, and pulled his head back even farther than it already was, making the boy cry out again. Growling, the older man said, "Boy, I warned you to obey me...and I warned you what the consequences were. I know you won't mess up again." He leaned in close to the boy's ear and was practically spitting at this point. "Because you won't be *alive* to." The boy started his final scream as the older man rammed his knife into the boy's groin and slowly forced the blade's path upward. The boy stopped screaming when the knife reached his sternum. Whether it was from shock or if a nerve had been cut, the older man did not know. He pulled the knife out, ignoring the squelching sound it made as his veiny fist tightened around the handle, and thrust it back in at the top of the boy's collarbone. This time, he did not stop the knife's ascent until it had reached the top of the throat, angling it under the bulky collar.

Now covered in the boy's spraying blood, the older man shook from some internal tremors. He held his boy close and kissed his red-stained lips. Pulling back and admiring the boy's lifeless body, he whispered contentedly, "Good boy...good boy..."

Outside in the dark, Max yawned again, stood up, spun in a circle, and curled back up to sleep for the night.

# 1

When Sean opened his eyes, it was because he finally had to take a piss. His eyes stared at the plastered ceiling with disgust. Two brown circles stained the ceiling right above the twin-sized bed, and he wondered whether a bad leak had happened upstairs at one point or a previous tenant of this apartment had decided to see how far they could toss a mug of coffee. As he pondered, he reached a hand under the lavender-scented sheets and scratched at his balls, but the need to piss was not to be abated.

He rolled out of the bed, stood, and stretched his sore body, the light from the window shining on his bare backside. He always kept the blinds drawn up so that people outside might "accidentally" see his naked form when he got up, but he never turned to look, enjoying the mere *possibility* that someone had seen him. Stepping over dirty socks, ragged jeans, boxers, and food-stained tees, he stumbled his way to the bathroom.

After aiming his cock at the toilet, he began pissing a steady stream, while his eyes stared blankly at the pile of towels hung above. It was a Friday, and he never had class on Fridays, meaning he never had a reason to get out of bed. Since his dad passed away four weeks ago, he'd felt even less reason to move, even when he did have class to attend.

Sean Wolfe was a senior at Southern Tennessee University, the dumbest school in the state, but it had been where his father had went to school, and his father before that, and his father before. As he finished in the bathroom, he wondered if his future son would attend this same school; he hoped not. "Sorry, dad, but I don't think so." He flushed and turned to face his tiny apartment.

He tried wrapping his mind around the fact that his father was still gone, even three weeks after the funeral back in Sean's hometown of Scottsdale. One heart attack out of nowhere, and the old man was just gone. Granted, it's not like Sean and his dad had ever been super close. Most of their time together was spent yelling, fighting, and regretting that they had even the same surname. Still, they were of the same blood, and Sean's dad had been the only masculine influence of any kind in his life. Sean looked up to his dad in his own way. Now that he was gone, his life seemed a little emptier.

He was not one to look back on his life, and he always made fun of his friends when they got in sappy moods of self-reflection. It was not that Sean personally thought such moods were undignified, but his dad had always hammered into him that it was effeminate for certain. When Sean had switched majors from chemistry as a pre-med student to philosophy hoping to be an eventual professor, his parents had almost disowned him for that alone, calling him a disappointment who would do nothing with his life. Threats of failure characterized his childhood, but now that he was in college, he was finally starting to question the standards by which he had always been judged.

The state of his room was one such standard; his sexuality was probably another. But despite all of this, despite the torment he had grown up with, now, he just felt depressed. His dad was gone, and not even the memories, flaming as they were, brought him back to life. He sighed and muttered to himself, "Well, time to get the hell out of here for a bit."

As he pulled a flannel button-up over his bare torso, he reached for his phone and texted Janie, "Hey chik-fil-a in twenty?" Janie, despite the fact that she had a vagina, was the one person who truly understood Sean. If there was anyone who could possibly distract him with good advice and food, it was going to be Janie. He scanned the room and found a pair of ragged jeans with holes in the knees and dirt around the ankles. Pulling them on, he fought to get the skinny jeans up over his cock and balls and struggled to button them properly across his little bit of pudge, but once he did, they felt comfortable, natural even.

His phone buzzed once. He leaned over the desk, swiped, and read Janie's response: "Yeah. Get a booth. Will only have a minute."

Smiling, Sean typed back, "Yes mam."

He found a pair of socks—mismatched though they were—and his sneakers before heading out the door, locking it, running down the stairs, and getting into his car, an old Dodge Intrepid with faded blue paint.

Campus was only a ten minute drive from the apartment, seven if there wasn't any traffic. Praised in brochures as the smallest campus in Tennessee, as if students equated "miniature" with "cute," STU seemed to have some grandeur in being what Sean thought the biggest joke in the state. All the same, he knew it could not be the worst in the country. After all, it had a Chik-Fil-A.

He pulled into its driveway and made his way inside, turning his phone's music app off now that he had arrived. The place still kept that old 80s diner vibe with its red-and-white checkered patterns. He looked around, watching the tens of students make their way through the diner with trays of food, but did not see Janie. So, he waited in line, ordered a sandwich and fries, and brought his food to an occupied bench after noticing the people there packing up their things. He smiled and nodded at them as they got up to go back to class.

He sat down at the still food-stained booth, spots of ketchup dotting the table; he felt his phone buzz in his pocket. Knowing it was probably Janie asking where he was, he pulled it out and saw it was from one of the dating apps, He4Him, notifying him of a recent message. His eyes scanned the diner to make sure no one was watching him as he opened the app and stared at the blurry but still explicit pictures of the naked men who had been messaging him since late last night.

He saw that four guys had messaged him. Two were fifty miles away, not exactly practical lays, and one was asking Sean to top him, despite Sean's profile description stating explicitly that he doesn't top. The final one, a guy named BBC4whtbttm, just had a profile picture of a long, thick, black cock. Sean clicked on it, his eyes fixated on the screen, and read the guy's stats: 36 years old, 5'11", 180lbs, and looking for a white bottom. Sean scrolled up and saw the guy was only eight miles away from campus.

"That's not too far..." he muttered, going back to read the actual messages.

"Hey boy looking?" the message read.

Sean began typing immediately when he noticed the guy was still online. "Yeah, u free? u host?" He went back to the home page as he looked up and saw Janie walking over from five or six feet away.

"Hey," Janie said as she sat down across from him. Sean fumbled to hide his phone and almost dropped it on the table for her to see his shame—and BBC4whtbtm's— but he caught it at the last minute and stuffed it into the pocket of his jeans, the phone's corner suddenly pressing into his erection. "Whatcha doing there?" she asked with a knowing grin, though Sean doubted she really knew.

"Nothing. Just uh...texting a guy from the frat party last night," Sean stumbled, his face flushing.

Janie sipped from a coke she placed to her right near the window. "Oh really? Was he cute? You guys...do anything?" She again gave him that sly smile.

Sean shook his head, never particularly wanting to talk about sex, despite his nightly ventures. "No, just been talking. What are your plans today?"

Biting into her own sandwich, Janie said between mouthfuls, "Well, unlike you, I have class today. And Mr. Mooney is a bitch, so I have to do my presentation today. And it's going to suck."

"You'll do fine."

"Maybe," Janie countered, swallowing. "But I swear he's out to get me this semester." She stopped and sipped from her coke. "So, anyway, how are you...feeling today?" She gave him a hard look, looking up over her glasses and trying to read his own eyes.

Sean looked out the window. "I'm fine. Things have been hard, but I'm fine."

She nodded, seeming to understand, and then said, "Well, you know you can always talk to me if you need anything. I want to be here to help you if you need it." She reached across the table and put her hand on his.

His initial instinct was to pull away. Right then, the only touch he wanted was a guy slamming into his ass. Affection did not make him feel better. The past few weeks that seemed to be all anyone wanted to give him: their condolences, their pity, their sympathy. He was tired of Aunt Mary trying to send him food, or Grandma calling him every day to check up on him. It made him sick. And Janie, for all her understanding and fun-ness, was sometimes the same as everyone else. "I'm fine, I said."

"Alright, loser," she said, standing up and grabbing her leather bag, "Well, I have to get going. Because some of us have class on Fridays." She left her empty glass and paper trash with a half-eaten sandwich there on the table, and came around to peck Sean once on the cheek. "You sure you're gonna be alright, Sean? You really do worry me sometimes."

He pressed his lips together and offered a smile. "Yeah, I'm fine. Go on to class. I'll message you later."

One eye squinted in suspicion. "Alright...love you, Sean." She turned and meandered her way through the crowded cafeteria.

With a sigh, Sean pulled his phone back out, noting the small wet spot on the front of his jeans and opened up He4Him again. BBC4whtbtm had left a response. Sean opened the full message: "yeah i host. 4219 fulton rd. get ur ass over here boy."

Sean swallowed as he typed back. "On my way sir." As he pulled up his Maps app, he stood from the booth, bumping his knee against the corner of the table and almost crying out. But he kept going, not looking to see if people had noticed his stumble. He tried not to think. He let his body just feel: this mixture of terror and desire. His heartbeat pulsed in his hands, his fingers jangled his keys in his pocket, and his eyes stared emptily through the crowd of people, lost in the toxic pull of his groin toward his car. He didn't hear the pounding of the rain on the asphalt as he stepped outside, and he didn't feel the icy drops pelting his face and neck. He felt heat, but he wasn't sure if it was coming from the GoPhone in his pocket or his member beside it.

As he stepped into his car, he made the conscious thought, *At least it's not a far drive. I'll be back before Jane is done with class probably.*

Shivers worked their way up his body as he drove through the rain and across the slickened roads. As they said back in Scottsdale, this wouldn't be his first rodeo. Even after having the sex for the first time a year ago, as a sophomore, he had already had sex more times than he could count. He always justified it by saying it was just part of the college experience. Most of the guys at the frat house bragged about their lays each night, always with a different girl. Sean was not much different—he just preferred the company of men: strong, muscular, dominant men.

Sean increased the speed of his windshield wipers and sighed. He thought back to when he had started doing this, when his dad died. He hadn't known any other way to deal with his grief. It was comforting in its own way, being used as someone's sexual object. He did not have to think or feel, and his very existence brought someone else joy, and guys *complimented* him on how good a bottom he was. So, it was a one-night stand every night, and he was surprised he hadn't contracted fungus on his balls or mites in his pubic hair. How would his dad react to his...memorial erection if he knew? Sean flinched. For his dad, "the gays" having sex was worse than an abomination—it was *disgusting*. For Sean, it was escape.

He passed through the downtown cityscape, making his way through six red lights before finally turning onto Fulton Rd, a street that had a CVS, a bank, a few used tire shops, and a small residential neighborhood.

"4215..." he muttered under his breath, lowering the speed on the windshield wipers, now that the rain had slowed and the wipers were starting to squeak against the glass, "4217...4219..."

His hands shaking against the wheel, he turned into the driveway, noting the foot-tall grass in the yard and the assorted car parts that hid among the weeds. While it's generally true that there are good and bad parts of town, Sean knew that even the good parts had the occasional trashy neighborhood, and this looked like one such case. As he got out and slammed the car door, he heard dogs barking in the distance, and he pulled the neck of his shirt up a bit to cover at least his neck while he walked to the door, straightening his back and shoulders. "Here we go..." he muttered, confidence creeping into his voice.

As the door opened, Sean admired the shirtless black man who stood in the entranceway, his muscles bulging from his abdomen and upper arms. Celtic tattoos wound their way across his ribs, and black gym shorts hung low on his hips, producing a V in the musculature of his thighs, ending at the lip of his shorts.

"What are you staring at, boy?"

Sean flinched at the deep voice calling him "boy," but he just murmured, "Nothing," all confidence drained from his own voice.

"Good," the man said. He looked around to make sure no nosy neighbors were watching and then grabbed Sean by the neck and threw him forward into the house. If the yard outside were to be any indication of the man's concern—or lack thereof—for appearances, then Sean should have predicted the disaster that awaited within the house. The cramped house had jeans, boxers, and hoodies covering the floor, so that Sean could not tell if he stood on carpet or tiled floor. The kitchen in the back seemed to have held more than one culinary explosion, with a tornado field of pots, pans, and what looked like scrambled eggs. The walls were cracked with holes every few feet the size of baseballs.

"Um, nice place," Sean said, struggling not to hold his nose to fight back the smell of rotten bananas that was coming from the kitchen.

He felt strong hands on his shoulders wheel him around and throw him onto a couch that had fallen through years ago. Sean gasped in surprise but did not get up, staring at the man as he pushed his shorts down to his ankles with the flick of a thumb at his waistband. The man's thick erection wavered in front of Sean's face. "So," the man growled with a husky voice, "what you into, boy?"

"Um..." started Sean, his face flushing, "just about anything. Uh...bondage...toys..."

"Bondage, huh?" the man said with a deep laugh. He turned around, giving Sean a good view of his muscled form and sculpted ass. The man was shorter than he had imagined, but he more than made up for it in physique. He was a solid hulk. The man bent over a box near the door and pulled out some bungee cables. "Let's tie you down then." The man smirked at Sean, and the sheer dominance made his cock harden in his jeans. "Strip. Then lay on your stomach, slut."

Sean did as he was told, placing his clothes neatly in a pile near one end of the bed, and he lay down as instructed. The man leaned over his face, turning lengthwise over the couch to get at Sean's ankles. His cock laid flat against Sean's cheek, and Sean could breathe in the man's musk. The scent alone was an aphrodisiac, but he did not do or say anything, trying to focus on what the man was doing to his feet.

The man struggled to secure the cables around Sean's ankles and the leg of the couch, through holes in the framework, revealing his inexperience at least with this. Sean just looked up at the man, eyes scanning the well-sculpted body. It was almost comical: this huge dominant figure struggling to figure out basic knots on a rope. If the situation were any different, Sean would have laughed. But he had learned early not to laugh at people who were fucking you. He could remember the slaps he had once received for that, and his cheeks remembered the bruises too. The man moved around Sean, and Sean felt him position himself on top of him. His eyes focused on the torn fabric of the couch, noting the stains—were they of food or sweat or blood?—and trying to disseminate the floral patterns beneath the stains.

Then, he felt pain as the man's cock impaled his rectum. He opened his mouth to cry out, but he clamped his jaws around the seat of the cushion, stopping himself. The man seemed to growl as he fucked Sean. He was a lot thicker than Sean had thought he was, and the guy hadn't even used any lube. Sean could feel his anus being torn and knew it had to be bleeding. This was hurting. But he did not cry out. Tears filled his eyes, but he stayed silent, letting himself be used until the man came.

·    ·    ·    ·    ·    ·    ·

Driving home, his eyes fixated on the road, his mouth hung open in a silent daze. The yellow lines to his left blurred, and he listened to the pounding of the rain on the roof of the car. Each pelting drop formed an echo in his head, a voice, an insult. *"Slut...slut...you deserve to die...slut...slut...such a disappointment."* This happened every time, of course. No matter what confidence or desire brought him onto the doorsteps of strangers, when he left, all possible doubt, misery, and self-loathing clouded his thoughts.

His parents had not been the type to go to church on Sundays, so it was not some religious shame he felt. In fact, when they watched movies as a family together, during the more mature scenes of R-rated films, his parents would tell his sisters to cover their eyes at the same time they told Sean, "Hey, keep your eyes open. You're grown up now. Watch it. You'll be doing this stuff soon." The thing was, at the time, Sean did not want to watch sex on these films. He did not like seeing women objectified like that. When he protested, his dad would buy him swimsuit posters and calendars for his room—to force him to face his sexuality. Only, Sean was not really comfortable sharing that back in high school.

When he started experimenting and learned he was in fact gay, things changed. He wanted to be sexually desired as much as the women dad had put pictures of all through their house. Having taken his fair share of psychology courses, Sean was familiar with the Oedipus complex. He had no conscious desire to be his dad's bitch. But still, he wanted to be the object of similar affections.

Affection...love...intimacy...sex...passion...these words flew through his head, pounding in time with the rain on the car. He didn't know what he wanted; he didn't know what hole he was trying to fill, other than the obvious physical ones. Everything felt empty. Everything inside felt hollow.

Finally, he pulled off onto the shoulder, turned on his emergency lights, and cried. Every three or four seconds, a car would rush past, splashing a torrent of water against his window, but he kept his forehead pressed against the top of the leather steering wheel, his tears and snot running onto its center. His face flushed as it contorted into blind rage and hatred. He hated himself, he hated his dad, and he hated that he didn't have the courage to end all of this himself.

A car honk startled him to reality, and a Mustang whizzed past. Sean looked up and wiped his eyes and nose on his shirt sleeve, then looked down at it in disgust. "Damn it," he said as he turned the car back on, pressing the power button on the radio before he continued on the way home.

He checked his phone as he drove, seeing a message from Janie: "Weekend finally!" Tossing his phone down, he focused on the road, no longer staring through the world and looking at it. He thought about what he would do tonight: what video games he would play, whose frat parties he would crash, which beers he would drink. Thinking of these things made him forget about his dad and BBC4whtbtm. Then, he heard the beep of his hookup app on his phone. His eyes looked down to the phone between in the cup holder between seats, but he did not reach for it. He turned the volume up on his music and drummed his fingers on the steering wheel as he drove home.

As he turned the key in the lock of his apartment door, he imagined what it would be like if his dad were waiting for him on the other side of it, stretched out on his couch or eating at his table. He knew that was not going to happen though. Even if it did, he didn't know what he would say. He could envision it: his father waiting on his bed, holding one of his gay mags, practically ripping it from the tightness of his fist around it. He would be pissed that his son had turned out to be a faggot. And that was one word that would have broken Sean. His dad had been disappointed when he refused to try out for sports in high school. He had been even more furious when he did some work with the color guard in the school's marching band. If Sean's dad appeared in his apartment, even back from the dead, it would not be a warm reunion.

Closing the door behind him, he kicked off his shoes, threw his shirt into the hamper in the laundry room, and kept walking into the living room, tossing himself onto the couch to turn on the television. His eyes watched the screen with no particular interest. It was some reality TV show, and the family on the show was talking about what Sean and Janie often called "white girl problems," such as Starbucks not having enough vanilla syrup for their latte, or having someone unfollow them on Twitter. His eyes grew heavy as he watched the melodrama with mild amusement, and then his phone made a beep, notifying him once again of a He4Him notification. He picked up the phone, not fully opening his eyes, read the words, "1 Message from Mason419," and turned the screen back off. "I'll message you tomorrow," he said to the empty room around him. He stared at the TV for a few more minutes and finally found sleep in the scene of one girl getting a scandalous manicure.

# 2

The next day, he met Janie at the Troy Community Bowling Alley, which sat between a gas station and a McDonald's. It had become "the usual place" for Janie and Sean, a place where 90s rock and pop music blared, blacklit stars and moons adorned the walls, and fries and a drink somehow cost eight dollars.

"The student deal, please," Janie said the guy working the register, a rotund teen with zits covering his face.

"Uh, that'll be fifteen dollars then. Need to see yall's IDs."

Janie and Sean flashed him their student cards, and they paid the fifteen dollars each. That gave them the shoes to rent plus unlimited games for the day. "Hey Sean," Janie started, "how has Dev been doing?"

"Oh, I don't know. I haven't talked to him in a while. Probably been parading around with guys in either arm," Sean said as he pulled on his shoes.

Janie nodded as she started fiddling with the 90s computer with its green pixels dotting a black screen. "Sounds about like him. I message him every once in a while, but he doesn't respond too often."

Sean laughed. "He'd probably say the same thing about me!"

"Alright," Janie said, standing up as the bowling balls came in through the machine. "You're up first."

He looked up at the screens above the machines, and he saw that she had named them "FAG" and "HAG." Looking over at her sly grin, he rolled her eyes, refusing to verbally acknowledge her joke. "Alright, here we go. My first one's gonna be a strike." He grabbed a 12-pound ball, held it up, stepped forward, and rolled.

Janie stepped up beside him and, watching the ball immediately roll into the gutter, said, "The only strike you're getting here is going to be a strike-out!" She hooted with laughter at her own joke, and Sean merely smiled, knowing he could be just as witty when she messed up next. He rolled again and knocked out three pins.

"You're up, ho," he said with a smirk as he went to sit down at the computer.

"Watch and learn," she called backward.

When he felt his phone vibrate in his pocket, he had a sharp feeling in his gut that he knew what that was. While Janie went up to bowl, he pulled out his phone and looked at it: "5 unread messages from Mason419." Sean muttered to himself, "This guy's persistent..." Glancing up to see Janie had hit two pins and was lining up her second ball, he clicked on Mason419's profile to take a look at him. He only had two pictures. One of them was a chest pic, with a leather harness tight around his shoulders and lacing his upper torso, showing off his muscular figure well; the other was a picture of his dick, average but hard. His balls were shaved, and a cock ring encircled them.

He quickly read through the five messages: "Hey boy"; "what are you doing later?"; "super kinky dominant MAN here. Been looking for a subby boy to give me some release whenever I need it"; "u interested?"; "willing to pay." Sean bit his lip as he looked back at Mason419's profile, trying to see if the guy seemed like a fake or not. He lived about fifty miles away, so he was probably in the country. He was older, 48 years old according to the profile. But if he was as dominant as he claimed, the guy could be worth the drive.

He shot Mason419 a message: "yes sir, I'm interested. Tell me more please."

Without turning to face him, Janie said in a cold, flat voice. "Are you going to message boys, or are we going to bowl?"

Sean almost dropped the phone in embarrassment, but he held on to it, flustered. "Yeah, um...hold on a second. I'm messaging Dev." He switched apps to his messaging app and shot Devlin a quick text: "Hey you free to talk tonight?" Devlin was one of Sean's few gay friends. While Janie was good for talking about just about anything, sex was not among those topics. He needed expert advice, and Devlin was just the guy to go to, along with being one of the classiest Lambdas in the university.

He stood to take his turn at bowling and managed to get a spare this time around. "Fuck yeah!" he called, and Janie glared at him.

"Showoff."

When he returned to his seat, he saw that Devlin had texted him back. "Yeah, at Lambda's tonight. Be there and we can talk about whatevs you need."

He smiled. "Hey Janie, looks like I'll be meeting Devlin at the Lambda frat tonight."

She turned and smiled, trying to hide the fact that she'd just thrown her ball in the gutter too. "That's great! Make sure you let me know how he's doing when you get home." She faced the aisle again as if she were about to roll, then turned back and said, "And make sure you don't get too wasted this time. I do not want a call at 2 a.m. asking me to pick your drunk ass up."

Sean pressed his feet together and saluted. "Sir, yes, sir!" Janie grabbed a heavier bowling ball and thrust it into his chest. He stumbled backward but held the ball with ease. "What was that for?"

"Being a dick."

He smiled and stepped up to roll again.

•   •   •   •   •   •   •

A couple of blocks down, he pulled into the parking lot behind the frat house. There seemed to be two types of Lambdas: the gay prudes, and the gays who fucked the prudes. Music filled the street from frat row, and there were so many people with red plastic cups outside that one couldn't tell who belonged to which frat. The smells of cheap alcohol and pubescent sweat drenched the air, and Sean loved it.

He walked out of the lot around the side of the building and looked up at the side windows. Most of them had curtains drawn, but some of them featured live scenes: a TV party in one room, a couple of bears making out in another, and some shirtless jocks dancing in the last. As he stepped out onto the main lawn, one group of guys called him over, but he shook his head with a smile. Another trio seemed to be playing a drinking game involving the lawn gnomes on the porch and a golf club. Sean entered the open fraternity house through the front door, passing under a hanging rainbow flag on the way and grabbing a red, beer-filled cup from a table past the doorway. Inside, Lady Gaga music blared through Bluetooth speakers tossed into every room, and gays of every shape and size mingled through the rooms. It looked like the start to a homoerotic Dr. Seuss book: One fag, two fag, head fag, new fag.

"Sean!" a voice called behind him.

He whirled around, and, and standing there in white and blue faded skinny jeans and a yellow, smiley-face-emoticon t-shirt (one size too small) was Devlin. The thin, bearded hipster waved Sean over with a grin. "Hey gurl!" Sean said as they hugged. "How have you been? It's been a few weeks."

"It wouldn't be so long if you actually texted me more often. Every time I message you, you say you're busy," Devlin replied with a smirk.

Sean shrugged. "Sorry."

Devlin grabbed Sean by the shoulders. "No, I'm sorry...I know you're going through a lot." He gave Sean a look of concern. "If there's anything I can do, let me know, yeah?"

Sean looked away, never sure what to do with that deep, serious look people had been giving him lately. "Yeah, thanks." He downed the rest of his alcohol and then picked up a cup that happened to be resting on a table beside him with no owner in sight. "Mind if we find somewhere a little more private?"

"Oh Sean!" Devlin said, a little too loudly for Sean's comfort. He leaned forward and grabbed the belt loops on Sean's sides, pulling him forward so their hips were touching. "I thought you'd never ask."

Rolling his eyes at Devlin's wink, Sean pushed him away, laughing. "Alright, faggot. You know this place better than I do." Devlin made the way through the glitter-covered crowd, holding Sean by the hand and leading him through the rooms, until they got to one of the private bedrooms Devlin had a key for. After they entered and Sean closed the door behind them, Sean asked, "So how many guys have you brought in here?"

"Let's just say there's a reason the carpet's white and not black, honey."

Sean grinned as Devlin sat down on the bed, gesturing for Sean to have a seat in the chair across from it.

"So...um...what did you want to ask me about?" Devlin asked as he leaned forward.

Sean pulled out his phone, debating on whether to actually show Devlin the conversation or not. "Well, you know I'm a bit of a freak in the bed, right?"

"Honey, I've seen your He4Him profile."

Sean blushed. "Right...so this one guy's been talking to me." Devlin raised an eyebrow. "He's quite a bit older, but he's into all the same things I am. Could maybe be a regular thing even."

"Have you guys hooked up yet?"

Sean shook his head. "No, we haven't."

"Well, what's stopping you? You usually don't come to me asking for permission to get laid."

Sean looked down again. "Well...the guy is way out in the middle of bum-fuck-nowhere. And he's even offering to pay."

"Um..." Devlin started, "seems a little desperate, doesn't he? That's a red flag, hon."

"I know, I know," said Sean with irritation. "But I think he's only desperate because he hasn't found anyone as...kinky and sub as me. I don't think it's the kind of desperation guys have when they're too ugly to get laid."

"How old is he?"

"48."

Devlin bobbed his head, considering. "That's not too bad then...Well, I'd say go for it. Just don't talk about the payment online. You don't want to get in trouble if he's a cop just fishing for you."

"Right," Sean agreed. "I know that."

"Then do it!" Devlin said, standing and clapping Sean on the shoulder. "Go have fun and get that cute twink ass of yours wrecked!" He said it with such a dramatic voice that Sean couldn't help but laugh.

"Alright. Thanks, Dev. I appreciate it."

"Don't mention it! I'm a good queen: I know what's best for my boys."

"Ha!" Sean called back as Devlin opened the door. "I haven't been one of your boys yet."

"No, you're one of my boys alright," Devlin said, winking. "Just not one of my bitches."

• • • • • • •

Back in the restless quiet of his own home, Sean heated up some leftover pizza slices and turned on the TV. He flipped the channel to a game show and tried to watch with at least some interest. As two contestants slipped further and further behind due to what seemed to be intentional idiocy—or maybe their accidental births—one contestant surged forward, brimming with confidence, intelligence, and no modesty whatsoever.

The harder he stared at the screen, though, the more his mind wandered. He first started thinking about his dad. What if he were still alive? What would he be doing right now? Usually on weekends like this, his dad would probably be out partying himself. The image made Sean flinch. For his dad, partying meant four things: drinking with a couple of friends, driving around yelling slurs at black people, fucking women besides his wife, and "trying out" whatever drugs he got his hands on. And Sean's mom? On a night like this, she would be worried at home, probably watching her stories on the television and taking some pills to help her sleep. When his dad got home, he'd probably yell at mom. He always found a reason. Usually, it was for acting weird, she in a drug-induced daze and not certain whether to accuse or let sleeping dogs lie, but he would bark some more and call her a fucking zombie.

Sean shook his head, realizing he was going down a dark road off Memory Lane, one he did not want to go down. He did not want to think about his dad right now.

With a sigh, he realized he could not even feign interest in the reality show and pulled out his phone, eager to read the next message from his admirer. When he turned the screen on, there is stood: "2 unread messages from Mason419." He opened his inbox and read the two messages: "Hey boy"; "why dont you come over tomorrow, and i can show you that im for real?"

Sean typed back, "Yes sir. What all are you into? You didn't answer me before?"

He looked back to the TV, but within a minute, the phone buzzed again. He looked down in surprise and saw his response: "same stuff you are in your profile: bondage bareback outdoors toys gangbang roleplay and even some things not in your profile. like ws pain and whoring my boy out".

With one hand holding his phone sideways on his chest, his other hand pulled the waistband of his shorts down enough so he could pull his cock out, the top of the shorts pressing under his balls. He heard his heartbeat drumming in his head as he started masturbating on the couch, his eyes staring long and hard at the man in the pictures, imagining this leather-clad man fucking him with that smooth, hard cock.

He typed, "Mmm fuck yeah sir."

Mason419 responded, "so what time can you cum tomorrow".

Sean felt heat rising in his blood. "What all are you going to do to me sir?"

"whatever the fuck i want boy. tie you down beat you breed you. whatever"

Sean winced at the bluntness of the guy, but he went along with it for now. "fuck yeah sir."

"tomorrow i want you to come in your best jock strap. Got it boy?"

"Yes sir!"

By now, he had been masturbating so hard he felt he was about to come. He read the next message, "and you're not allowed to speak until i tell you so, got it? What time you coming?"

He cried out as he shot his seed onto his stomach and chest, lying there with half-lidded eyes and a sense of euphoria over him. After half of minute, he licked his lips and looked back at his phone.

"b there at 4 sir."

As he passed into sleep, he was only vaguely aware of the cheers coming from the game show on the TV or the occasional buzzing his phone made, and he had no way of knowing it would be the last night he would get to sleep on his own couch.

# 3

As Sean left the city behind, his usual trepidation became wonderment. When he usually went hiking in Tennessee, there were bustling parking lots, overweight tourists, and large-print signs informing readers that, yes, this indeed was the right way to this beautiful-landscape-made-tourist-trap. But here, the wilderness was *wild*. Although it was daylight, the slender trees managed to block out much of the sunlight, casting reds and shadows across the woods. The road itself was just a narrow dirt path, full of jarring bumps and rocks that left Sean glad he had bought new tires recently.

That morning, Sean had gone through his usual routine and asked Mason419 for the address. The guy had provided the address as well as full directions. They seemed simple enough: take the Interstate, get off at exit 374, turn right on Webber Street, then another right on Chickasaw Road, and take that until you can turn off onto an unmarked road right after the bridge. At the end of that road would be his house: 419 Chickasaw Road. Sean remembered thinking that the guy had to be old and country if he didn't know that everyone had GPS of some kind nowadays. Still, with each mile he traversed the wood, another bar of service vanished. It made him nervous. He had never gone *this* far just for sex.

He knew there were risks in fucking a different guy each night. Just having a regular guy—even if it wasn't a romantic relationship—would be safer for him that what he had been doing. In the heat of the moment, in the sweat of the bed, he felt content. It wasn't sexual euphoria, not by a long stretch. If he were doing this because it was just a fun activity, he would simply be hypersexual. But it was deeper than that. Being tied down, being told what to do, being called a bitch and a slut, he derived the greatest pleasure from being able to please these men, being able to bring *them* sexual euphoria. He did not crave intimacy or passion; he craved that feeling of utility. The feeling that he mattered, even if only in that moment.

He slowed down as he came to a bridge that went over a shallow ravine. The bridge was formed from just large gray rocks and mounds of gravel, so Sean really had no choice in his speed—three inches to the left and the car would be in the water. As the car bumped and shook over the bridge, Sean began regretting his decision to come out here...even if it was for a good lay.

He stopped the car once he reached the other side. A quick glance at his phone showed he had plenty of time—still thirty minutes to four, and the GPS said he would be there at a quarter till. He opened the door and stepped out, holding his phone to his chest. Out in the distance, he saw the ravine emptied out into a small pond. There were a couple of rotting park benches around the pond, and Sean wondered if it had once been a popular fishing spot. He held his phone out, opened his camera app, zoomed in, and took a picture of the pond. His thumb hovered over the Share button, and he wondered whether he wanted to have to explain to Janie that he was going out to the middle of nowhere to have fetish-based sex with a guy he'd never even met, when—for it was a matter of when, not if—she saw the photo. Sighing, he pressed Cancel. When he returned home, he'd probably upload it on his computer and just change the privacy options so she couldn't see it. That was just not a conversation he wanted to have. Pulling his jacket around his thin frame to fight back some of the wind, he entered his car again and continued down the dirt path.

As the car bumped and rocked, he wondered what Janie was doing then. He knew she worried about him all the time, but he also knew she would worry twice as much if she knew half the things he did in the dark.

After a few minutes, small square cemetery appeared on his right, and he slowed down again, noting the small, hand-carved tombstones that marked roughly ten graves. He came to a full stop, wondering whether he should get out and pay his respects. Sean was by no means a sentimental type. He had fucked in graveyards, no less. But since his father had died, he had found a new admiration for them, if not respect. He checked his phone, neither service nor data out here, and saw he was still pretty early and had plenty of time to make it the rest of the way up the hill to the guy's house.

Stepping out of the car, he pocketed his phone and walked around the front of the car to look into the graveyard. A three-foot-high fence surrounded the area, and, now that he was up close, he noticed that all the graves were small, either a pet cemetery or lots of buried urns. He leaned over the fence to get a close look and saw that each of the flat grave markers had two numbers, a number from one to eight that took up the majority of each stone, and what seemed to be the year of death. Yet, there wasn't a birth year.

"Unless..." he muttered. "These were...infant deaths?" The thought of eight buried babies in front of him with little more than a number designation repulsed him, and he stepped backward with a groan. "What the hell..."

He got back in his car and continued driving, trying to drive out the morbid thoughts of the graveyard. Still, he couldn't shake the shivers that now worked their way up his spine. He was not sure if these came from the impending hookup or the child-sized graves that loomed behind. Driving on, he struggled to bury these thoughts. Yet, he couldn't help but notice the graves lacked the sentimentality one would normally expect of grieving parents.

Shortly after the cemetery, he came to a barn. Its red doors were closed, but he could occasionally hear the whinnying of a horse from inside. This far out in the country, he suspected they had to belong to Mason419. The doors looked new, their bright red a contrast to the paintless walls and boarded windows.

*The guy's a real handyman alright, but it would be such a bitch going to town for supplies...* Sean observed.

Generally, Sean liked to consider himself an outdoors person, insofar as he liked to hike popular trails, walk around the zoo, and bike through town—again, all *controlled* wilderness. But he had never really encountered horses outside of seeing them in pastures he drove past or in movies. So now, in the middle of the woods, unable to use his cell phone, with an old barn and a creepy cemetery, he suddenly felt claustrophobic, as if the woods were trying to choke him, as if he were the one trapped in the barn and not the horses.

He did not stop the car to stare too long this time, aware that he only had a few minutes till four now. He knew he had to be getting close by now. With his eyes trained on the rearview mirror, he watched the barn, a red smear against the dark horizon, until it faded from view. When he focused his eyes ahead again, he slowed the car down suddenly, eyes widening.

He saw it: a two-story house with walls so white, it looked as if someone had taken an eraser to the background of the scene. Yet, the house's pointed roof looked menacing, a dagger reaching upward to pierce the belly of the canopy. Long tendrils of thick ivy wound their way up the sides of the house, and a few of the windows had been smashed in. If it wasn't for the light in a couple of those windows, Sean would have thought it was one of those abandoned houses that urban explorers dream about. It had the shape of a small church, the way its bottom floor spread out and its top reached a sharp pinnacle; yet nothing about its appearance seemed holy to Sean. Perhaps in former years, it had been a church—the cemetery would explain that much—but now only the birch trees were its captive congregation.

He looked at the mailbox with 419 on a sticky note and MASON in all capital letters beneath that. He noted with a smirk how odd it was for someone to make their hookup profile username their real last name plus their house number. And that little bit of ridiculousness made him forget his current situation for a moment. The car wound along the fence and behind a rusted green truck, a Ford Ranger from the 80s with tree trunks and branches scattered in the bed. Dents marked its sides, and one window was completely smashed in. Still, the tire tracks in the dirt showed it had been used recently. Sean had always felt bad about his 90s Intrepid, but when parked beside this country behemoth, his looked like a top-of-the-line sports car.

Sean turned off the car and sat there, looking through the fence at the small country house and its surroundings. Being a philosophy major, Sean had often connected his studies with the real world...as he perceived it. One paper topic he had always tossed around as a joke would be the connection between gay guys and the things they kept in their yards. If Mason419 had been mentioned in the paper, the leading observation would have been that the man lived a simple life.

The yard was mostly dirt with small patches of grass poking through here and there. A few landscaping tools dotted the yard: a wheelbarrow, what looked like a plastic hoe, some potted plants by a corner of the house, just waiting to be planted in the dirty of the yard. Sean's eyes made their way back toward the mailbox, and that's when he saw the doghouse.

Finally, he got out and closed the door, not bothering to lock it—who here would come and break in to his car?—and started to approach the doghouse. It looked handmade, the wooden planks with nails halfway sticking out at all of the corners and the roof two simple boards laid down on top of the rest of the house. Black paint above the entrance spelled out the dog's name: "MAX."

Sean saw a German shepherd lying down in the entrance to the doghouse, his ears perked and his eyes watching Sean closely. Its fur was a mix of browns and blacks, and its winter coat was starting to come in. Sean stopped a couple of yards from the doghouse and called, "Hey Max, who's a good dog?"

Max raised his head, looking at Sean with excitement.

"Yeah, are you a good boy?" Sean now leaned down in the dirt, his knees crunching the leaves, and held out a hand toward the dog.

Max ran over, tail wagging, and pressed his head under Sean's hand, demanding to be petted. Sean laughed and rubbed the back of Max's head, between his ears. "Yeah, such a good dog," he repeated in a soft voice. As the dog rolled submissively against him, he noted how soft the dog's fur was, how young and playful it was, and how eager it was for attention.

"He likes young guys," a gruff voice called behind him.

Sean spun around, face flushing, and stammered, "I-I'm sorry. I'm a uh...big dog person."

The man laughed. "Good. Means you two will get along great." He looked a lot older in real life than in his pictures, yet he seemed no less attractive. He wore a plain black t-shirt that was tucked into a pair of working jeans, dirt stains and holes running up his legs. A black leather belt kept his pants tight around his waist, and the matching black sneakers on his feet were half-caked in dirt themselves. He was bald, but he also had a thin mustache that curled down around the edges of his mouth.

Sean smiled weakly.

"Did you find the place alright?"

"Yeah," Sean said, going back to petting the dog. "The way up was beautiful, too." He agreed at first, then thought of the eight compact graves back in the cemetery.

"Good, boy. Now, come on inside. Looks like it's about to rain anyway."

The man headed back inside, and Sean stood, leaving the dog whining for more attention. He looked up at the sky and could barely make out the shades of gray in the sky above. Sean followed Mason inside, noting again the vines that curled even around the steps to the front door.

As dirty as the outside was, the inside was a complete contrast: immaculate, dusted, and without much decor at all. Scanning his eyes along the room, he saw a black leather couch, a television on a stand, and a few floor lamps, spreading orange light through the room. "Um...nice place."

"Excuse me?" Mason snarled behind him.

"Oh...um..." Sean flustered again, realizing his mistake. "Nice place, *sir?*"

"Good boy."

"Thank you, sir."

Mason closed the door behind them and turned to face Sean, veined fists on his hips. "Alright, boy, if there's one thing you'll learn about me, it's that I love rules. I'm a stickler for them." Sean swallowed but stared at the formidable man. "Doing a good job gets you rewarded. Disobeying gets you punished. Understand, boy?"

"Y-yes, sir. As long as you don't go past any of my limits." Sean had few limits, including pain, anything that left a mark on him, blood, shit, stuff like that. He had made sure to communicate those before setting off this morning, but now, faced against this Goliath of a man, he felt the need for the slightest reassurance that those limits would be respected.

Mason's eyes grew cold and hard, and he advanced three steps—his boots thudding into the carpet—and swung an open palm into Sean's face, and he fell backward onto the couch.

As Sean looked up at the man in fear, nursing his reddening cheek, Mason kneeled in front of him and snarled, "And rule number one is don't talk back to your master, boy. I'll decide what your limits are." He grabbed Sean by the arm and hauled him up. "C'mon."

Sean regretted coming here. He wished he had confirmed the rules outside, in a relatively neutral area. But now, not even he could deny his raging boner pressing against his leg. But he was too scared now to do anything about it. He could only hope that this would be over quickly; he would promise to be back soon and immediately block the guy's number once he was out of the driveway. He followed Mason up the stairs. At the top of the stairs was a bare bedroom: white walls, white carpet, and a queen-sized bed in the center. There were no adornments on the walls or even lights besides the overhead fluorescent lights, an odd touch for a country house.

"Get on the bed," Mason said. "I'll be right there."

It looked like one of those hotel beds: white pillowcases, white sheets, white comforter. The bedframe and headboard were black themselves, and Sean noted the chains attached to each bedpost, ending in a leather cuff each. He swallowed a little nervously and sat down in the center of the bed. He didn't want to seem too comfortable and lie down before he was told what position to be in.

He heard scuffling downstairs, and he found himself shaking, terrified of this present situation. Still, Mason had said he'd be fine as long as he didn't break of any of these rules he spoke of. Sean wished he knew what all the rules were. At least, he knew he'd be safe if he followed orders to the T. He stroked his cheek where the man had slapped him, a red promise of more to come. He considered leaving, but he knew the man was probably trustworthy. After all, he had been left unattended, even if just temporarily.

Mason finally appeared at the top of the stairs, but now he was a different man altogether. He wore a leather harness around his chest, and chaps of the same material cradled his thighs, leaving his groin exposed and pale, his erection throbbing and pointing toward Sean threateningly. "Get undressed, boy. Slowly."

Sean swallowed again and grabbed the tail of his shirt, lifting it up and over his head. He did not like the momentary obscuring of his vision, but he tried to do it slowly enough to please Mason. When it was off him, he placed it neatly on the bed beside him and started to take his shoes off, then his socks. His eyes focused on Mason, who now leaned against the wall, nursing his erection with his right hand, his fiery eyes staring at Sean with a wolf's hunger. Sean unbuttoned his pants and peeled them off, making careful effort to do it slowly, feeling each fold of the jeans rub across his skin. Next came his jock strap, too, paying attention to the fact that Mason had said all his clothes had to come off. He felt ashamed. Never one for wearing underwear unless the guy demanded it, he usually enjoyed the liberating sensation of his balls in the air. But now, naked before this beast of a man, he felt as if he were being devoured in that longing gaze.

"Good boy." Mason finally approached, and Sean leaned back out of instinct. Mason pressed a hand against Sean's chest, pushing him flat onto the bed, and then he threw Sean's clothes down to the floor beside the bed. He crawled onto the bed, his harnessed chest hovering over Sean's, and he pressed his face against Sean's, kissing him with a mouth that threatened to eat him. The man's breath tasted like cheap cigars and even cheaper beer, the dark smoky scents mingling with the heat of alcohol. But Sean did not protest.

As Mason began humping against Sean, his cock pressing into his, Mason hissed in Sean's ear, "So boy, you got a girlfriend?"

Sean's eyes opened—realizing that he had had his eyes closed during this forceful humping—and he replied, "No, sir."

"A boyfriend, then?" Mason snarled, gyrating his hips harder, rubbing Sean's own cock raw.

"Yes, sir," Sean lied.

"Oh, a little faggot boy then?"

Sean closed his eyes and inwardly glared at the man as he whispered through clenched teeth, "Yes, sir."

"Well then, makes it all the funner to steal you away, huh?"

"What?" Sean blurted.

Slap. The blow left a reddening mark on Sean's other cheek this time. "Don't you question me, boy," Mason growled, staring hard at Sean as he sat up and crawled over Sean's body, now sitting on the top of his chest, his cock pressing into Sean's mouth. "Suck that cock, boy. Get it nice and wet."

Sean was more than willing to oblige if it meant he didn't have to talk. As Mason began to fuck his face, Mason leaned over, grabbing something from beside the bed. He turned back and held a small brown vial. "You take poppers, boy?"

With Mason's cock still in his mouth, thrusting over his tongue, Sean could only hum around the length, knowing full well that Mason would not care if that was agreement or refusal.

Mason held the open bottle under one of Sean's nostrils and with another hand held the other nostril shut. "Breathe that in, boy." Sean obeyed and then did the same with the other nostril. "Good boy." Mason put the bottle back where it was beside the bed and picked something else up. When Sean heard the rattle of the chains, he knew what was next. He felt his right hand placed in a cuff, clamped tight around his wrist. Then, Mason moved to the other hand, his cock pushed in odd angles in Sean's mouth—Sean struggled to not let his teeth graze Mason's cock; that could not go well—so that Mason could bind Sean's other wrist as well.

"Faggot boy like getting tied up?"

Sean hummed.

"Good boy. You know, I've had a lot of boys before. But never a faggot boy." Sean kept his eyes closed but frowned. What was Mason even talking about? From Sean's perspective, Mason was as much a faggot as he was. "I have a lot of straight buddies over all the time. I'll have them take turns with your ass. Maybe fuck all your holes at once. How's that sound?"

Sean didn't hum this time.

"Maybe I'll have you stay around here as my houseboy. You won't be allowed to wear clothes. You'll service any guy I bring to the doorstep. You'll service anyone and anything."

He pulled out of Sean's mouth, allowing Sean to finally take in deep breaths.

"You suck good, boy. Let's see how tight that ass is now."

He got off Sean's chest and positioned himself between Sean's legs, lifting each one so that the underside of the knees rested on Mason's shoulders. With a grunt, he thrust balls-deep into Sean, who cried out instantly, face scrunched in pain. "That's right, boy. In this house, the only lube you'll need is your own spit. So make sure you make my cock wetter in the future. You'll learn that quickly."

"Yes...sir..." Sean managed through his clenched teeth, anger being replaced by his blinding pain and terror. The poppers were starting to kick in finally, and he felt their wave of numbness overcome him, about twenty seconds too late.

"Do you work, boy?" Mason said as he worked his cock in and out of Sean's ass.

*God, this guy talks a lot,* Sean thought. "Yes, sir."

"Where do you work?"

"I'm a student, sir."

"What are you doing wasting your time there?"

Sean opened his eyes and gave Mason a confused look but said simply, "I...don't know, sir," scared of what other answers could have brought.

"You can be my houseboy," Mason repeated. "I'd give you food, water, a home...You wouldn't need anything else." His thrusts grew faster and harder. "You want me to come, boy?"

"Yes, sir," Sean said, finally feeling relief at knowing the end was in sight.

"Alright, here I go, boy." The man's face turned purple, making his head look like a wrinkled beet, and he began grunting ferociously. "Here it is, boy." He arched his back and tilted his head up toward the ceiling as he snarled a final time. Sean felt Mason's hot seed spill into him. He felt the man's poison fill him, and he hated it. *At least he did come quickly...* Sean thought gratefully.

Mason relaxed after a few seconds and untied Sean's wrist, the intensity in his features suddenly absent, revealing what looked like a gentle old man. He reached a hand under the bed. "Here," the man growled, handing him a plastic cup with water. "For the poppers."

Sean chuckled weakly, grabbing the cup with a shaking hand, and said, "Yeah, probably a good idea before I drive...sir." It was only halfway full, and he downed it quickly.

As he waited for the haze on his senses to dissipate, he asked—more to break the awkward silence than out of genuine interest—"So, do you think you'd like me over again, sir?"

"Oh, sure, boy. You'll do well."

The response sent that jolt of fear through Sean's heart again, and he set the cup down beside him. "Uh...good, sir." After a few seconds, he tried again, "So, how long have you lived here?"

"Whole life. I work back in town though. Do some handiwork here and there."

"That's cool," Sean ventured, testing to see if not saying "sir" was acceptable now.

"I enjoy it enough," Mason said with a smile.

Sean smiled back, and he closed his eyes halfway, reveling in that exhaustion he usually felt after sex. *Well, he seems nice enough when he's not sex-crazed*. Despite the violence of the encounter, Sean wondered if maybe this wouldn't be so bad. Mason didn't seem so crazy when he wasn't engaging in dom-sub roleplay, so maybe this could work out.

He yawned and said, "So, do you have guys over here a lot?"

Mason looked down as if suddenly embarrassed. "I did a couple of months ago, a regular, cute boy like you...but he died."

Sean's eyes opened only halfway. "I'm sorry to hear that. That...that...sucks..." Sean was never good with condolences, struggling with receiving them as it was. His eyes started to close again, and then it hit him. He forced his eyes open as best as he could, realizing five minutes too late that he had been drugged. "What...why..." he managed, noticing that he was slurring his words.

Mason grinned and knelt beside the bed, pulling something black and thin out from under it. Sean tried to crawl away to the opposite side of the bed, eager to leave but his strength quickly leaving his body. "No..." he muttered. He felt something hard and cold close around his throat, and he heard a clip from it. Then, his world faded to black.

# 4

Waking up slowly, Sean felt like he needed to puke. Through blurry eyes, he frowned at the startling new world around him. The shapes came first: a circular window in the wall above his head, the rectangle of a door in front of him, the square of the bed on which he lay. His head swam as he tried to focus on any one thing. Smells started to register in his mind: sweat, cum, even the acrid smell of nail polish remover. Next came the sound of rain beating on the window.

"What...what the fuck..." he managed, his tongue dry and swollen in his mouth. He tried to swallow and felt his Adam's apple press back down against an obstruction. Reaching a shaking hand up toward his neck, he traced his fingers along a hard metallic ring that encircled his throat. At the far left and right sides of the band, the metal bulged, as if encasing something thick and rectangular beneath. It was tight around his neck, not constricting his breath, but he was unable to pull it from his neck. He fingered a spot on the collar that must have been a keyhole and groaned.

Memories came floating back, piece by piece. Janie...Devlin...the hookup app...driving in the country...the river...the cemetery...the barn...Max...and then Mason. His eyes widened in horror. "I was...drugged?" His head still pounded, and he felt dizzy. "What the hell did he do to me?" He did not try to move though. His eyes adjusted to the dim light, noting the shadows of the raindrops hitting the window against the wall near the doorway. Sean had never been a smoker, but he felt that, if he were, now would be the time for a serious smoke. He became aware that a light was coming from the doorway, from downstairs.

"My clothes..." he said, scanning the floor for any sign of his garments from the day before. He crawled out of the bed and felt his head swim from the sudden movement. He kneeled on the carpet, cradling his head in his hands. "What the fuck did he drug me with?" After a full minute had passed, he turned to look under the bed. Nothing was different: a bottle of poppers, the chain-and-leather restraints, a couple of towels, and even a few sex toys. Groaning, he turned toward the doorway. One foot at a time, he made his way in its direction.

His body stumbled into the wall at the doorway, and he breathed heavily as he rested there, staring down the stairway, now seeming to be twice its actual length. He swallowed dryly again as he pressed the back of his head against the cool wall. *I need to get my clothes,* he thought. *And get my car keys and get the fuck out of here. Then, I'm going to call the police on his ass.* He nodded to himself. He had a plan of action. Now, nothing could go wrong.

With a groan, he pushed himself off the wall and toward the stairs. With one hand on the rail and one hand on the steps, he worked his way down each carpeted stair, his legs sometimes crawling, sometimes sprawling. He was more scared of slipping and falling headlong down the stairs than of passing out where he was. The fibers of the carpet scraped and burned his legs and palms, but the pain felt numbed, probably from whatever drugs Mason had given him. As he worked his way down the stairs, he noticed a small red hole in the crook of his arm, the skin around the vein red and swollen. "He...gave me an...injection?" Even his words were slurred, he realized, his ears awakening more to the sounds around him.

When he reached the bottom stair, he sat there and just focused on keeping his breathing even. After a few minutes, he grabbed the railing and raised himself up. Fingering the collar at his throat, he glanced around the living room. The furniture was exactly as it had been the day before. The floor lamp cast long shadows throughout the room, and the TV's darkened screen reflected Sean's naked form. He noted the thick collar around his neck, for that was indeed what it was. He swallowed and called out, his voice shaking and hoarse, "H-Hello? Is anyone here?" He licked his lips. "M-Mason?" His voice fell flat, drowned out by the storm outside. Still, the house was small. If Mason was still here, he should have heard Sean by now.

He looked back around the stairs. He noticed a hallway that led further back into the house. With a hand pressed against the wall for balance, he walked down it. The first door on his left was open, revealing a large bathroom: a white porcelain sinktop with the usual toiletries, a circular tub near the back window, an overhead shower with a glass door, and a toilet, lidless. Beyond that, a bedroom extended to the right, dimly lit like the living room, with classical Greek paintings of cherubim and gods decorating the walls and red curtains enclosing the four-poster bed. Across from it was an open entranceway with a set of stairs leading down into what was likely the basement. One more opening remained at the end of the hall. As he approached, he heard running water.

Sean slumped forward against the last entranceway, opening up to a kitchen, lit like his bedroom, with fluorescent lights set in the ceiling. Like most of the house, it too was white in its every corner: the countertops, the walls, the cabinets, the pantry door, even the microwave and oven. Then he saw it.

There on the kitchen counter, beside the running tap, lay two sheets of paper, one slanted across the other. He swayed as he lumbered over to them. Pressing both his hands against the counter for balance, he stared hard at the top sheet. It had inked handwriting scrawled on its surface. "Alright, fucker, what's going on here..." he whispered as his eyes scanned the sheet:

Dear Boy,

Welcome to your new life as my houseboy. Lucky Boy #9. There are some rules laid out under this sheet, and I expect them to be followed at all times if you want to avoid getting punished. In case you're wondering how I actually intend to keep you here, it's simple: your collar. It is a shock collar that has the strength of about a cop's taser. Around your neck, that will knock you on your ass and knock you out. The basic perimeter is fifty feet from the house. That's where the invisible fence is. I've locked up your clothes and stuff in the basement. If I ever catch you tampering with the locks down there, you might find yourself locked down there, too.

I am heading to town to take care of some work, but I will be back this evening. Help yourself to anything in the fridge or pantry. Make sure you read the rules below this sheet before you do anything hasty!

Be a good boy while I'm gone.

Your master

Sean's hands were shaking now. He reached one up to the collar around his throat and tried to pry his fingers under it, but it was too tight, not allowing even that inch of thickness between it and his neck. He felt suddenly like he couldn't breathe, like his lungs could only suck in half their usual air. "Fuck!" he yelled, refusing to believe this was actually happening to him right now.

He looked down at the next sheet, his heart racing. In bold, capital letters, the title read, "RULES." His stomach churned as he remembered what Mason had said the previous afternoon. "You've gotta be shitting me." Below the title were ten numbered rules, all starting with the words, "You will…"

He swallowed and read:

RULES
1.   Boy is to make sure the house is clean and dinner is ready by the time Master gets home.
2.   Boy is to be naked at all times.
3.   Boy is to service any men who come over in any way that he can, but he shall not address any of them as Master.
4.   Boy is to always address Master as Sir.
5.   Boy does not speak unless spoken to, does not look at Master unless told to, and does not leave Master's side unless told to.
6.   Boy is not to try to leave the perimeter of the fence.
7.   Boy is not to try to remove his collar or try to fight his Master.
8.   Boy is to obey all of Master's commands.
9.   Boy is to make sure he is clean, inside and out, at all times for Master's use when he is ready.
10. More than a partner or a spouse, Boy is to love his Master.

Half of the rules seemed like practical jokes-serve any guys that came over; being naked at all times—the other half psychotic—cleaning the house and obeying every command, without limit. Each one of the rules brought questions, fears, and doubts to Sean's mind, but the last one struck the hardest. "More than a partner or a spouse," he repeated, each word a stutter on his lips, "Boy is to love his Master." He suddenly felt like he had been thrust into some fucked up "Beauty and the Beast" retelling, and readers were expecting him to fall madly in love for his captor, Stockholm style. And that feeling, the idea of eyes watching him, him in his naked form with only a shock collar around his neck, tears running down his eyes, and all his senses betraying him, sent shivers down his spine.

A low whine rose in his throat. His mind ran in all directions. He could not see this as actually real. This was criminal and illegal. Mason couldn't expect him to stay here indefinitely, could he? Then, a memory stirred in him. "The letter. Mason had said I was number nine..." He remembered the cemetery. "There were...eight graves..." His eyes widened as he realized that the gravestones had not marked infants or pets but Mason's previous captives. "Holy *shit*," Sean moaned through a hand.

His mind, sharpened the slightest by adrenaline, worked through as many solutions to his plight as it could.

*I could call Devlin...No. My phone's locked up in the basement, and I haven't seen any phone in the house.*

*I could try running...No. My car keys were in my pants pocket.*

*I could try fighting back...No. I haven't seen so much as a pair of scissors with which to stab the guy...and he's a lot stronger than me...and will probably expect me to try  And I can't do much since I'm fucking drugged.*

He was cut off, isolated from the world as he knew it, and no knew he was here. Neither friends nor family. *Still*, he thought, *people would notice I was missing*. They'd send police...But he had left no sign with anyone as to where he was going. He had told Devlin about Mason—though he hadn't told Devlin his name—but there was a good chance that Mason had already taken down his profile now that he had caught his prey.

He could see the headline now: "STU Senior Goes Missing After Father's Death." Though he could bet on the headline playing off his family like that, as if he had committed suicide through grief or depression, Sean imagined his not-so-familial father standing in this old, white house with him, shaking his head, calling out to him, "You did this to yourself, Sean. You were asking for it. And you got what you wanted. You got
what you deserved, faggot."

"No, Dad," Sean whispered, denying him, denying everything. "No matter what you thought, I don't deserve to fucking *die* here. I don't deserve for this crazy ax-murderer to chop me into pieces and bury me in a shallow grave, unmarked." He clenched his fists and shook his head, dismissing the image of his father before him. Instead, he imagined what would happen when Mason returned home.

He refused to believe this nightmare was real. And like many terrors, this was one he had to run from.

He ran to the door and opened it, the chill of the rain sweeping over his naked skin, each drop an icicle that pierced his senses. But he didn't care. He had no intention of staying here, and he would run to town naked if he had to. The dirt yard had become mud through the torrential downpour, and Max had managed to work his way on top of the doghouse, Snoopy-style, seeming to prefer the rain to the mud, just as Sean was preferring the rain to the house himself.

As his eyes scanned the yard, he saw his own blue car still parked in the driveway. And he desperately wished now that he left his keys in the car before exiting. However, in front of his own car, Mason's green Ranger was nowhere to be seen. The path, mud though it now was, was a stark contrast of brown against the green of the forest; almost inviting Sean to try it. He steeled his will and moved.

Once he started walking through the mud, his bare feet squelching and slipping in the mud, Max looked up and barked. Sean was not sure if Max was being encouraging or warning, but he ignored the barks. He tried not to think at all. He kept his arms wrapped tight around his chest and his head low to keep the rain out of his eyes, and he walked.

Still, with each step, he estimated how many feet he had walked. *Five...ten...fifteen...twenty...* He was past the front gate. Smiling to himself, he picked up the pace, still estimating numbers and gaining confidence with each step through the mud. *Thirty...forty...fifty...*

He did not reach the number sixty. He heard a loud beep coming from the clamp around his throat, and he was vaguely aware of a prickling sensation there. And as volts of electricity shot through his neck and crackled through his body, he struggled to push forward, inching his way up the hill and hoping the battery wouldn't last forever. Then, in his last moments of awareness, he tried to step backward, back to the invisible line. His mind hit an instant reset, and he would not be conscious again for another several hours. His body crumpled backward into the mud while the cold rain beat down upon him.

# 5

Cold water hit Sean's face, and his eyes snapped open, not fully aware that he had even been unconscious. But now, instead of rain beating on him in the woods, the cold water of a shower sprayed onto him. He gasped in shock and pressed himself against the grime-encrusted wall. The freezing droplets pierced his senses, and he screamed, not really vocalizing any words in particular, his feet and hands pressing against the tiles and the wall, trying to create distance.

"You're gonna stay in there until you're clean, boy."

He stopped screaming at the sound of the deep voice. The bass sent a spike of fear into his gut, and he realized instantly where he was though not what had happened. Sean worked himself into a corner of the shower and edged his way up against the wall, turning the water's switch to Hot. His whole body ached as if he had slept in a million wrong positions. "What...happened?" he said over the spray of the shower. Speaking, he felt how sore even his throat was.

"I warned you in the letter: shock collar. You only have about fifty feet away from the house. And of course you tried running anyway, like a bad boy." Sean kept his mouth closed, trying to measure Mason's tone, a mix of anger, scolding, and a bit of amusement even. He wondered if Mason had ever heard himself, how absurd his words sounded. The type of masculinity and dominance Mason exhibited wasn't something Sean had thought still existed. "You're lucky though. The first boy didn't have that collar. His wasn't waterproof. He died the first time it rained. I found his dead body still spasming like he was having the best orgasm of his life."

*He died...* Sean repeated in his mind, no longer questioning how ridiculous Mason sounded. "You're not serious about this, right?" he said in a flat tone, not wanting to seem aggressive or in any way dominant. "Like...do you want money? A car? Anything?"

Mason laughed, a deep chuckle that echoed through the shower. "No. All I want is you. Your body is perfect, boy. Now, I just gotta train you so your behavior is perfect, too."

Sean was silent for a moment, considering his next reply. He closed his hands into fists against the wall, feeling the futility of them. "So...I'm stuck here...forever," he said, hoping Mason would correct him with "until the end of the week" or "until the end of the month" or "until the end of the year" even.

"Yup. Forever," Mason affirmed. Sean could hear the smile on his face in that rising tone. Shutting off the water, Sean heard Mason say elsewhere in the bathroom, his bass echoing off the walls, "You know, boy, I'm going to have to punish you for breaking some rules. You know that, right?" Sean winced. If what he was experiencing was to be the *norm,* he could not begin to imagine what *punishment* would be like. Through the glass door, he could make out Mason's silhouette, a dark shape against the light over the mirror. And the shadow stayed there, waiting for a reply, *expecting.*

Sean pressed his forehead against the wall, trying not to break down crying in the sheer helplessness of his situation.

He heard Mason sigh, as if relenting. "Boy, if you have any genuine questions, now is the time to ask. From now on, you are my boy, my pup. If there's anything you don't get, say it now...or forever hold your peace." That word again, "forever," it felt like a low chime in Sean's head, like the ring of the last nails being hammered into the coffin.

Opening his eyes, Sean worked his jaw, testing it. "Will I...Will I ever be allowed to leave here?"

"Maybe in a few months. If you're good, I'll take you to the park or something."

"What about..." Sean's eyes darted, seeking some form of hope in the stains on the wall, as if he expected a small door that would lead him into Wonderland hidden under the filth. "What about school?" He grasped at straws, anything that might make Mason rethink this whole scenario.

Mason laughed again, and Sean half-slumped against the wall, his laugh as tremor-inducing as the collar had been outside. "What do you need a degree for? I'll give you all the professional training you need."

*Of course you will, fucker.* Sean faced the door and realized suddenly that all his freedom—his dreams, his plans, his hopes—were all gone now. The most he could hope for was that someone would realize he was gone and that the FBI or something would be able to find him. Still, the fact that eight others preceded Sean as Mason's slaves did not bode well for his chances. "Alright," Sean said, his voice almost a whisper. He opened the shower door and looked down at the tiled floor, refusing to look up at the man with his jeans and tucked-in shirt leaning against the bathroom door.

"Alright, what?"

Sean winced. "Alright, *sir*."

"Good boy," Mason said with a smile, his lips tight against his face. He straightened from resting against the sink and looked Sean up and down, as if appraising him. "I want you to go grab your sheets from upstairs and wash them. Stuff's in the basement." He saw Sean's arched eyebrow. "You need to start on your chores. Here's a list of them," he said, pointing to a few sheets of paper by the sink. "We're going to be having company in a few days, and I want this house—and the yard—spotless."

"Company?" Sean repeated.

Mason opened the door and was halfway through it when he said, looking over his shoulder at Sean, his blue eyes piercing. "Yes, boy. Company. Your Master has friends over most weekends. And we try to be good hosts, don't we, boy?"

"Yes, sir," Sean replied, grabbing a towel and drying off. Mason walked out, leaving Sean alone to see himself in the mirror. There was a ring of red both above and below the shock collar and another spot of red on his arm, where Mason had undoubtedly injected more drugs into him. Then, his eyes looked through his reflection, not even aware of his form. *This can't be my life now. It just can't.* Maybe he wasn't like the other eight. He had family that loved him, friends that checked on him daily, and a university that might even feel liable for his disappearance. But still, all of that was out of his hands. There was nothing he could do on his end.

After grabbing the list and then going up to get his sheets off his bed, he went downstairs to start on the chores Mason had given him—*He sure does like his lists*—and looked around the basement for the first time. A washer and dryer sat rested against one side of the basement, moisture and mildew staining the wall behind it. As Sean looked around, he saw several pieces of sex equipment: a sling, a stockade, even a full sex machine. The devices turned the simple basement into a dungeon, and Sean wondered if any of the previous boys had ever been trapped down here, left overnight in a stockade or strapped down to the sex machine while Mason went to work.

The thought gave him shivers, and he started putting his sheets in the washer, still looking around as he did. In one of the back corners, toward the stairs, he saw a pile of metallic boxes, each with a lock on them. After he started the washer, he walked over to the stack. Each one was marked with a number, one through nine. He realized then that each of these probably contained the personal belongings of Mason's boys. Would this be his fate? In a few years to have only a locked box in a basement and a two-square-foot grave in the woods? Both marked by a number, his name forgotten?

*No,* he told himself firmly. *I don't know how yet, but someone will come for me. They'll find me.* He kept repeating this as if it were a mantra, and he went upstairs to work on chores, something to occupy his mind and distract him from his new situation. As he worked, he tried not to think. Mason always seemed in the corner of his vision, but the task at hand stayed in the forefront of his mind.

Each day went the same for the rest of that week. When Mason drove off to work, Sean would get up and work on the chores list. Many of the items on the list were long-term projects, like repainting a side of the house, growing plants in the yard so it wasn't just dirt, and replacing the windows. As he worked outside, Max would sometimes come over and demand to be petted, but Sean felt distant, as if it wasn't really him living in this strange house, serving his even stranger master. As Sean pet the German shepherd, he would marvel at the dog sometimes. The dog seemed like any other he had ever met: energetic, playful, and loyal. When he thought of people like Mason having a dog, he envisioned just these growling and snarling pit bulls and Rottweilers that had to be secured to a post by a three-foot chain. But Max was nothing like his master. And for that, Sean felt a little less alone. There was at least something warm and familiar here. "We'll get out of here, Max. You and me both." He felt stronger with the dog at his side. A boy and his dog on a mission. But not even that connection could keep him from the monotony of the days.

Each day felt the same, mindless and silent. When Mason asked him a question, Sean responded as shortly as possible, always remembering to add "sir" to the end of his response. He would eat small meals like sandwiches or Ramen, as Mason kept the pantry and refrigerator fairly stocked. Each night when Mason came home and sat down to watch the TV, Sean brought him some simple meal and sat down on the floor beside him, doing as Mason told him, occasionally rubbing his feet or sucking his cock, but it rarely moved past that. Mason didn't try to start many conversations with Sean. After all, it was clear to Sean that Mason had no interest in Sean's past: Sean was to be Mason's object, a slave and servant. One night, the most conversation the two had was, "Hey, have you been a good boy today?" "Yes, sir." "Good boy!"

So it was that the days passed by in a mindless blur. Each night, Mason came into Sean's room and injected the drug into Sean's arm, and Sean welcomed the numbing bliss. In the reaches of his mind, he worried. Was he becoming addicted? Where was Mason getting his needles? Were they even sanitary? But in the moment, those thoughts were far. Whatever the drug was, it made him calm, made him not think, made him not feel, and that was a blessing in itself. It made the time pass so much quicker.

On Saturday—Sean knew it had to be Saturday only because Mason didn't go to work that morning—Mason approached Sean in the kitchen with a metallic anal plug the size of Sean's index finger. "Boy, put this in. I want you to wear it all day."

"Yes, sir," Sean said as he put the plug in his mouth, lubricating it with his saliva, before he pressed it into his ass.

When Mason was sure Sean wasn't going to ask about it, he continued, "Our company is coming today, boy, so I want you to make extra sure the house is spotless. No dust. No stains anywhere. And make sure you're nice and clean, too." He put a rough hand to Sean's chin and tilted his face upward. "Listen close, boy. I put a razor in the bathroom. It's an electric one so I think I can trust you with it. I want you nice and smooth, you hear me? If I see one hair on your body, except the top of your head, I'll cut it off with a knife. And you'd better believe I won't be gentle."

Sean swallowed. "Yes, sir."

"Good boy," came Mason's automatic response with a smile, and he patted Sean on the butt, almost fondly, as Sean turned away.

Sean crossed back to the hallway and entered the bathroom, closing the door behind him, appreciating even this mild privacy—there was not even a lock on the door. He turned on the shower before going back to the counter where the electric razor sat. It was black and sleek, plugged into the wall yet showing a green light, indicating it was fully charged. *Company...* he repeated. *Maybe someone will realize how crazy Mason is, and they'll call 911.* He thought about ways to communicate to these men without Mason knowing he was doing so. Yet, despite Mason's obsession with lists, there did not seem to be pen and paper anywhere in the house—Sean had looked—and nor was there a computer for him to type things. Sure, he thought, any substance could work: ketchup on a paper towel, sticks in the yard...but each option posed the risk of Mason also seeing the message, and that thought seemed worse than staying here complacent forever.

He shaved, and double-checked and triple-checked to make sure there was not a hair on his body. He found himself performing near contortionist maneuvers against the sink so that he could see in the mirror every inch of himself. With the image of the small cemetery firmly planted in his mind, he had every confidence that Mason would follow through on his word with the knife if Sean disobeyed.

As he stepped out of the bathroom, dry and smooth, Mason passed him in the hallway on the way to his bedroom. Mason looked back, his eyes again appraising Sean. "Good boy. Now, start some dinner for my friends."

"But sir," Sean protested, forgetting himself, "it's only like two o'clock, isn't it?"

A tinge of red crept into Mason's face, but his tone stayed level, "Yes, boy, it is. It'll be an early dinner. People will start coming around four, and you'd better make something *good*."

"Yes, sir," Sean said, turning and heading to the kitchen, anger rising in him too. Serving Mason sexually and with chores even was one thing; becoming a professional cook in two hours was another. With neither cookbooks nor the Internet at his disposal, Sean knew he had to stick with what he knew: how to make Ramen taste good, how to microwave soup, or how to make a couple of his family's recipes without cheese. He had wandered into the kitchen a few times already, hoping to find something that could be used as a makeshift weapon, but almost everything was made of plastic or rubber, and he wasn't even sure he would have the strength to use one of those to effect.

He glanced through the refrigerator for cooking ideas. Feeling confidence in the principle of cooking something until it looks like it's burning, he settled on cooking chicken and pasta. The time flew as he made garlic butter for the pasta as his mom usually did and burned the chicken lightly as his dad usually did. The rich scents quickly filled the kitchen, and Mason occasionally came in to tell Sean it smelled great, but Sean always responded with "Yes, sir," refusing to even look Mason's direction. When it was done, the time on the clock high on the kitchen wall read only 3:30, and Sean sighed, keeping the food on low heat until Mason's company arrived. He called out to Mason, who was probably in the living room at the end of the hall, "Sir, dinner is ready!"

Mason called back, "Then come out here and wait with me."

Sean ground his teeth but headed toward the living room. Mason was sitting back in the leather couch, a beer can in one hand and a languid look in his eyes as he stared at the television, watching some crime show with mild interest. Sean sat down beside the couch and watched with him, uninterested and nervous for the company, wondering if he would have a way to communicate the need for the cops to be called. After a few minutes, Mason looked down at his phone and typed on it, smiling. He did this every once in a while for the first episode.

Halfway into the second episode, they heard the first knock on the door. Mason looked up from his phone toward the front door and said, "Go and answer it, boy."

Half shaking already, Sean stood and crossed over to the door, his bare feet patting against the hardwood floor. *Here we go,* he thought. *My rescuers.* When he opened the door, he saw two guys standing there: one an older bear type with a t-shirt too small for his stomach and gray hair that covered his head, face, and double chin; and the other a short and slender middle-aged man with thick black hair protruding from his low hanging collar, a paradigm of what went wrong in the eighties.

The first looked at Sean's neck and reached a meaty hand toward his throat. Sean stepped back, and the man stopped. "Hey Mason," the man called, his voice thick and slurring. "Is this one not even trained yet?"

Sean heard Mason stand and approach, but Sean did not want to take his eyes off the two strangers. The other one simply stood there, hands in his pockets, and smiled. "Not yet," Mason responded, now at Sean's shoulder, smacking him on the ass. "Boy, go back to the kitchen and get some plates ready. I see another car pulling in anyway."

"Yes, sir," Sean said, blushing.

"Come on in, guys," Mason said, gesturing with an arm for the two to enter.

Sean walked as quickly as he could to the kitchen, ignoring the voices behind him and pissed that the men so immediately saw him for what Mason saw him: a boy. He was not sure in retrospect if the large man had been reaching to touch the collar or strangle him, but it was still an invasion of personal space—Sean sighed—whatever that was anymore.

As he prepared the third plate, Mason stepped into the kitchen, placed his rough hands on the kitchen island across from Sean. "Hey, the others are here. With me included, that's six plates."

"Yes, sir," Sean said, grabbing more plates from the cabinet.

Mason gave him a hard look. "Boy, I know this is a lot of change for you, but you can say more than 'yes, sir.'"

Sean almost responded with the "yes, sir," but instead said, "I will try, sir."

"Good boy. Now, get those plates out here."

As Sean brought the plates out to the living room, he observed the company fully. Mr. Large was probably the most boisterous of the bunch, eager to cram food in his mouth, the garlic sauce splashing against his face and catching in his mustache. Mr. Slender was much more reserved, barely touching his food and just watching the others with an amused glance. Two black men sat on a chair beside the couch, one in the other's lap, and they chatted mostly with themselves, occasionally pretending to acknowledge that Mr. Large was still speaking. One of them was shirtless, revealing a small but muscular chest, with low-fitting gray sweatpants. The man underneath was much stockier, built like a football player, with a button-up shirt and jeans. The pair seemed, in Sean's mind, to be trying out for the roles of Beauty in the Beast in an upcoming gay African-American adaptation. A final guy, probably about Mason's age but with a more

50

prominent disinterest plain on his face, stood and leaned against the doorway, chewing a wad of gum as he read from his phone. Once all the plates were set, Mason waved a hand dismissively, sending Sean back to the kitchen in case he was needed.

He stared through the kitchen window, noting how dark it was becoming outside, the pinks of dusk fading through the trees, transforming to violet. After a few minutes, Mason called, asking for beers all around. When he brought them, he went on and picked up the dirty plates, mostly eaten, and the party seemed to ignore him at this point. They had started to play a game of cards, and, though he wished he could at least stay and watch, Mason again shooed him away. Halfway to the hallway, Mr. Large called, "Hey *boy*," he said the word with such force, Sean was sure he was going to spray beer through his nose, "you got any chips back there?"

Sean turned back and growled through his teeth, "Yes, *sir*. One moment." He went and fetched the chips, hearing the laughter at his back. That was how the party started.

Much to Sean's embarrassment—visible by the increasing red in his face—he realized he was becoming the men's naked serving boy, bringing them beers when told or getting them refills on chips. Though no one really said anything about him as they ate and played their cards, they felt no hesitation at the occasional, "Boy, refill, now." These other men had no problem seeing Sean as the object Mason had told him he was now. Whatever hope Sean had felt in rescue from Mason's company was becoming lost with each passing minute, their laughter a bold affirmation of his invisibility—and inhumanness—to them.

Halfway through one card game, Mason called Sean over to him. "Would you like another refill, sir?" Sean said, expecting it at this point.

"No, boy," Mason said, stepping up to Sean with a beer in hand, the liquid still audibly sloshing inside the can. "I want you to go up to your bed and get on all fours like a good boy."

"No," Sean said, red rising in his face, partly in anger and partly in denial that he was going to let this continue. He could not meet Mason's gaze, not wanting to see the anger that was probably on his face, but instead looked at the others in the room. Mr. Large had a grin that rivaled even Mr. Slender's, and the black couple shared an expression of surprise, their mouths forming large 'o's and sharing glances, the unspoken thought being one of disbelief. The guy against the door had stopped chewing his gum and for the first time regarded Sean with interest.

However, Mason did not explode on him, at least not verbally. The man's hand clamped around Sean's neck, right above the collar, his thumb and middle finger driving into Sean's pressure points, and Sean cried out in pain, his face scrunching. Suddenly, he was moving, Mason guiding Sean up the stairs with that lock on his neck. Sean cursed as he was led up the stairs, tripping often but never falling. Finally, forced through the doorway, Sean was thrown onto his freshly made bed. Vaguely, he heard the thump of footsteps as the other partygoers made their way up the stairs, but his senses became overwhelmed as Mason adjusted the restraints on the corners of the bed, one hand clamping back on Sean's neck to keep him from moving and the other working the restraints around Sean's limbs. At one point, he had to let go of Sean's neck to get to the other side of the bed, and once he let go, Sean tried to move. He realized the mistake instantly when Mason punched him hard against the side of his head; stars and colors swarmed Sean's vision as he fought to stay conscious. This time, he did not even feel his other hand and ankle restrained. He only became aware slowly that he was on all fours on the bed. A cushioned cube, like a small footrest, had been wedged under his chest, so that only his hands and legs touched the bed. His head and ass were well in the air. His head still reeling with pain, he was vaguely aware of the forms around him.

Now, forced to do as he was told, he begged silently for a blindfold, any way he could not see his tormentors, not see their faces, and not reveal his tears and shame. He wanted to disappear, to fade. He wanted to close his legs together, but Mason had attached a metal bar between his ankle restraints, removing even that smallest comfort. As if his blessing were heard, one of the men pulled a blindfold out of his pocket and forced it over Sean's face, turning the dark world even darker. Sean felt a smack on his ass and knew what was in store for him at last.

They began their night of pleasure and his of pain. They did not simply take turns with him as he might have hoped; they did it in pairs: one in his mouth and one in his ass; two in his ass; one in his mouth while another used a toy in his ass. It became a game to them seeing how many ways they could fuck Mason's boy, and each load of come they filled him with became a tally mark in permanent marker, supplied by Mr. Slender, on Sean's left ass cheek.

At one point, Mason pricked Sean's arm with a needle, and Sean felt the warm pressure of the drug being forced into his veins. It was the best feeling he had experienced all night. Numbness flooded him, and time became irrelevant. His vision created shapes and forms in the darkness of the blindfold, and his senses blurred. Words met his ears, but he was no longer sure who said them or in what order.

*"The boy has no limits."*

*"Can I fuck his ass and then his mouth?"*

*"You like that cock, boy?"*

*"Hey Tom, get a picture of that ass!"*

*"Use your beer for lube, then!"*

*"Fuck, his mouth is too dry now."*

Then, at least two hours later, even blindfolded, he noted one man's touch; it was different from the others and shocked him into awareness from his drug-induced state. The hand, smooth and a pleasant contrast to Mason's rough, callused hands, rubbed up and down his ribs, much like how one might rub a horse's side. "Who's a good boy?" the man's high voice cooed. He sounded older, one of those grizzled queens who were the sweetest uncles you could ever have but the kinkiest freaks in bed. "You are, aren't you, boy?" It was the guy who had chewed his gum, leaning against the door. Sean knew it.

He moaned softly around another guy's cock, his first sound that wasn't of pain the entire night.

"That's right," Mr. Gentle said. "I'm gonna ride your ass for a bit now, so relax. Be a good boy."

Sean felt the guy who was fucking him pull out, and Mr. Gentle leaned over Sean, putting a hand on Sean's back as he positioned his cock with Sean's asshole. He slowly slid it in and gasped as he did, Sean moaning with each inch. It wasn't that this was *romantic* or *sweet* to Sean. But it was sensual. "You alright?" Mr. Gentle asked, and Sean nodded. "Good." Once he was fully inside, Mr. Gentle, leaned the rest of the way over, his chest pressing against Sean's back and started to ride him.

Mr. Large called out, "Fuck yeah, break that ass!" A few others mumbled their agreement, and Sean became aware that everyone sounded exhausted, though not as much as Sean himself was. Mr. Gentle fucked him, slowly at first but with increasing intensity and rising need.

Before even five minutes had passed, Mr. Gentle whispered in Sean's ear, his mouth breathing hot air into it, "Alright boy, I'm going to come. Are you ready?"

Sean gasped and replied with an embarrassing need of his own. "Yes, sir."

He felt the heat spread inside him as Mr. Gentle bred him. The colors and shapes started to leave Sean's vision, and he realized the drugs were starting to wear off. He had no idea how long he had been under, but he knew it had been more than the usual dose. Mr. Gentle lay there and panted softly in Sean's ear, now exhausted himself.

"Alright, guys, that's it for tonight," Mason finally said, with a voice dominant enough that even the partygoers knew to obey. As Mason walked everyone out of the room, everyone except Mister Gentle, Sean relaxed onto the bed, lying flat. Sean heard them scuffle out of the room and down the stairs. He heard the front door open and final pleasantries being discussed.

"You—you did good, boy. What's your name? Your real name?" Mr. Gentle asked, his voice still a whisper.

"I'm Sean," he said, a surge of hope filling him.

"You know," Mr. Gentle said, nuzzling Sean's neck with his nose. "You're pretty good at this. I might have you over my place sometime. If you'd like that."

"Yes," Sean responded instinctively, eager to accept any way out of here. "I'd like that very much...sir."

Mr. Gentle laughed. "What? You don't like it here?" He kissed Sean's ear.

"I...I..." Sean stumbled, not sure how safe it would be to say he wanted out as soon as possible.

"It's okay, boy. I'll talk to your master. I'll see what I can do."

Mr. Gentle stood up, pulling his cock out of Sean's ass with an audible pop. "Thank you, sir," Sean responded, his voice soft but still loud enough to hear.

After getting dressed, Mr. Gentle pulled off the blindfold and put it in his pocket. "Hey..." Mr. Gentle said behind Sean, still out of his range of vision. "I'm leaving a note for you between the mattress and box spring. Read it when your master goes to work, alright, boy?"

"Y-Y-Yes, sir," Sean stammered, tears in his eyes, the final culmination of his exhaustion, shame, terror, and now hope.

"Good. Until next time, Sean."

As Mr. Gentle walked out of the room at last, Sean felt the weight of that piece of paper between the mattress and the box spring, like a pea between the mattresses, a seed of hope that gave him discomfort all through the night, despite his exhaustion. He half-wished Mason would just drug him again and make him not feel anything. He was too awake, too aware, and still restrained to the bed when Mason called out to him from downstairs, wishing him good night as he went to bed himself.

# 6

Sean waited until Monday when Mason returned to work before checking under the mattress for the letter Mr. Gentle had left. As he sat up, he noticed two things that were different that morning: his head was pounding as if someone had driven a nail into through his skull, and there was a small syringe full of a clear liquid on a wooden stool beside the bed. Under the syringe was a handwritten note. "Fuck," Sean muttered. "Fuck him and his lists and notes." His eyes squinted as he concentrated on the paper.

*Hey Boy, I think I trust you enough to let you take your own drugs. I'll refill this twice a day. But never more. And only if you behave. And I don't need to tell you not to get any ideas about using this on me. When you're done using it, put it on the table in the living room. If I come home and it's not right there, I will know, and you won't like what I'll have in store for you.*

Sean clenched one hand into a fist while the other picked up the syringe. Having grown up with a rural South background, he had received all of the drug education he could ever need. The dangers of weed, meth, crack, and even over-the-counter meds had always been in the annual curriculum, from middle school through high school. So, naturally, almost all of his friends had at least experimented with most of those drugs. But Sean himself had stayed away. He knew enough that he realized he was already experiencing addiction symptoms. With a shaking hand, he aimed a needle at one of the veins in his forearm, as he had seen done in the movies, and pumped the liquid into him. It hurt like hell, more than when Mason did it.

He sat there for a few minutes, eyes closed, trying to minimize any movement for fear of it upsetting his head further. Nausea crept its way into his stomach, and his fingers grasped the edge of the mattress as he rode the wave, concentrating only on not vomiting.

Once it passed, he exhaled, opened his eyes, and slid off the edge of the bed to the floor. He pushed a pale hand under the mattress and felt the crinkled paper of Mr. Gentle's note brush his hand. His heart rose in his chest as he pulled it out, careful not to rip it.

He unfolded it and read it aloud, mouthing each word softly, "Would love more time with you, Sean. Maybe just your master, me, and you next time? Talk to him about it. Mention the sixth boy to him. Be a good boy. Dustin." Just as quickly as his heart rose, it sunk. Mr. Gentle / Dustin was just wanting to use him as a sex object as much as Mason. "Fuck!" Sean called out, confident that no one could hear him.

Then, his eyes widened, an idea forming. While Dustin might not be his direct way out, maybe it would be a way to soften Mason's defenses and create an escape route all the same. Even as he felt the drug start to kick in, waves of numbness washing over him and relaxing his stress, he loathed the pleasure it gave him. "The bastard did get me addicted." In the silence of the house, his own voice was a small comfort. With no one to talk to but Mason when he came home, Sean was his own—and only—friend.

He grabbed the emptied syringe and worked his way down the stairs. Raising his other hand to his neck, he felt the collar. The skin beneath it still stung from his single runaway attempt, but he could not reach under the collar to scratch that itch. He was most aware of the burden when he tried to sleep. The drugs usually helped, but some nights, he'd wake up, feel the heavy weight around his neck, and stare through the darkness at the ceiling and wonder what Janie and Devlin were doing now. Had they called the police yet? Was he in the news?

Once he made it to the bottom of the stairs, he placed the syringe on the table and looked out the window, just to confirm Mason wasn't here. Once his suspicions were proved correct, he smiled. Yes, he would soften Mason's defenses. If he played the "good boy" card, maybe he could get certain freedoms, be allowed further range of movement, maybe get the collar removed and sneak a message out to someone. It was something, a definite plan of action that he could work toward, and his rage would fuel his every act. That rage would get him out of this personal hell.

Over the next few days, Sean worked on his chores with a new intensity, pouring all his effort into the work. He knew that clearing out the entire list would always be an impossibility, but at least it gave him something to do, and it would show Mason that Sean was being complacent and *trying* to be a good boy. That simple obedience might just work.

Naked but the collar, he handled each task with determination. He worked on replacing the windows, re-painting a side of the house, giving Max a bath, and even taking care of some of the vines that had wound up the side of the house. His motivations aside, the work was comforting. It gave him ways to pass the time, and he enjoyed turning this house of horrors into something even he could be proud of. He took pleasure in his work outside, and spending time with Max usually made it even better. Sometimes, the dog would sit a few feet away and just watch Sean attentively. Other times, Max would come and curl up at Sean's feet like a cat. When this happened, Sean would usually take a break and pet the German shepherd rather than moving to continue his work. The dog was a companion, and at that moment, companionship mattered more than anything else. Max was someone he could trust.

Of course, bettering the house was only a start for what he had in mind, but he knew that even with his current plan it would take a while before escape would be an opportunity. He kept thinking about that day though: how he would make it out of there, find a way back to school, still make it in time to take his finals, have Mason arrested for the rest of his life, get some media interviews, be paid thousands to write a memoir of his experiences, and be known as *that* survivor. He felt guilty for the thought: achieving fame for his discomfort. But still, even that thought gave him hope. Being a survivor meant he would make it through this. It's an old riddle he had discussed in a philosophy class early in college: after a plane crash, where do you bury the survivors? You don't. They're still alive. Though the memory made him smile at first, the more he thought about being buried, the paler his face became. What if they gave up trying to find him? What if they had a funeral for him, not knowing he was only a few miles from the school? What if they had a gravestone with his name and the date of the last time anyone saw him inscribed there? It made him feel like being buried alive...Then, he thought of the gravestones just a little ways past his shock collar's range. Would he be among them if he fucked up soon?

He tried to avoid these thoughts and focused on the work. He had no answers to the questions. With anger burning in his mind, he worked each day and served Mason each night, ever obedient. Sometimes, Mason would sit on the couch and watch TV, usually a sports program or a sitcom. Other times, he would tell Sean to lie on his stomach on the couch, and Mason would fuck him. Doing it this way was a lot easier than the first few cases of being tied up forcibly. Despite the entire lack of consent, it felt less like rape, less violent anyway. But Mason's company was bearable this way. Sean always had a smile on his face, with plans to manipulate Mason always in his mind. Hatred brewed inside Sean, and that hatred gave him some hope. By the end of the week, his plan seemed to be working.

That Saturday, Mason asked Sean to join him outside after breakfast. It was a simple enough request, and Sean followed him out with a smile on his face. As they walked down the stairs, Sean glared at the back of Mason's bald head, thinking, *It's working. He believes I'm actually learning to like it here.* He felt his heart race despite the Downer working through his blood.

"Hey boy, I want you to help me extend the fence out some." He handed Sean a pair of thick gloves and one of two post hole diggers.

Sean looked out past the wooden fence to the grassy area beyond, and his heart froze. "Um…" he started, remembering what had happened the last time he had walked past the fence.

Mason laughed and put on his own gloves. "You've been good this week, boy. As a reward, I've extended your range a bit on the collar. Not much, but a little. Just to show you that I reward good behavior."

Sean offered his best smile, trying to act the "good boy" through his clenched teeth. Instinct begged him to raise the post digger and slam it into Mason's head, yelling with each stroke, "I used to have unlimited movement, you asshole!" But he knew he did not have the strength or the energy. He was drugged, and Mason was stronger. If he failed, Mason could—and probably would—kill him. He simply said through his smile, "Thank you so much, sir." He made it sound as grateful as he could. Then, he remembered what the note said. As he stood a few feet from Mason, digging where Mason had pointed for him to dig, he asked, "Um, sir, can you tell me about…some of your other boys?" He kept his eyes down on the ground, making sure not to scissor off his toes with the post digger, and he was just as mindful not to pinch his dick against the handle either.

Mason looked up for a second before thrusting the post digger into the ground, pulling up a huge clump of grass and dirt, then returned to looking down. "What do you want to know?"

"Um…" Dustin hadn't told him what to ask about, just that he should find out about the sixth boy. "Just tell me little things about each one…sir."

"Alright, boy." Mason stopped and placed his hands on top of the post digger, leaning over it while Sean still worked on his hole. "Well, I told you what happened with the first one. That was about fifteen years ago, probably about this time of year, too. Picked him up off the streets. He was hitchhiking and homeless. But I guess he preferred not having a place. He tried running end of the first week."

"And was shocked to death."

Mason looked down, his jaw slack. "Yeah…he died. Even though it was the quickest death of all of them, it was probably the hardest for me."

Sean watched his expression closely. Mason genuinely seemed sad about it. How fucked up was this guy?

Mason continued, "The second was a guy I bought. He wasn't worth the price though. He couldn't even wash fucking dishes, the kid was so spoiled."

"You…bought him, sir?" Sean asked, trying to sound captivated out of interest rather than terror.

"Yeah," Mason said with a smile, showing his teeth as he stood up straight. "There are probably…twenty or thirty guys in the state who trade around. It's usually homeless guys they take. Sometimes, kids volunteer themselves into the market." *The market?* "Means they don't have to worry about getting a job or a house. Don't have to worry about shit with family. And buyers usually take care of their property." *Is that what I am now? His property? Like a car or a house? Like a piece of furniture?* "But when your property doesn't work right, you throw that out and get a replacement. Killed him in his sleep. Lazy fucker."

Sean swallowed. "What about the next one, sir?"

Mason sighed. "Number Three was gorgeous. A great fuck, too. My friends, some of the ones you met last weekend even, loved that ass. But he wasn't a good houseboy either. After two months, he ended up overdosing on the benzos and killed himself. Number Four was a runner. Tried four times, just like his name. So, I cut his legs off." Mason paused, letting that sink in.

Wincing, Sean looked down, unable to meet Mason's eye now. He stopped with the hole and said, "Um...wow, sir."

After spitting on the hole he was working on, Mason said, "Damn right. I work my ass off in town to put a roof over you kids' heads and food on your plates. I never hurt you unless you deserve it. And how have some of you repaid me? By running." He shook his head. "Fuck no...That's not how things work. I learned though. Made the shock collar stronger. Number Five...another good fuck. Obedient, too. And he loved the horses. He was the first one I extended the collar range for. Those horses killed him though. He had never been around them before."

Sean had a graphic image of being tied down in the barn with horses trampling him down, stamping their hooves through his ribs, into his head, as if it were a hairy pumpkin, the gooey contents splashing against the hay. "What about...Number Six?"

Mason gave a short laugh and started working on his hole again, grunting. "Well. That right there was my trophy boy. Had him for two years. I loaned him around the market here now and then. Even to one of the guys you met last weekend. Number Six liked being a little slut. But he was good and straight. Maybe more masculine than me even—"

"Straight?" Sean said with a laugh of his own. "Let himself be fucked by a hundred guys, and he still called him straight?"

Pausing in his digging, Mason's eyes sent icicles into Sean's. "Boy, watch yourself. Being a faggot has nothing to do with fucking. It's how you act. You're the first faggot who's ever been in my house, and you better not let my friends know that. When they're here, you be a good boy. No girly shit."

Sean clenched his teeth, wanting to lecture Mason on sexual identity, gender expression, and homophobia, but he stayed silent.

"He died though. He killed himself. Even as my trophy boy, I walked in one day, and he had hung himself. In the bedroom where you sleep now."

Sean could imagine it now. A graying corpse hanging from the window, eyes bulging, flesh rotting. Like something out of the movies.

"Number Seven loved his drugs. He stayed quiet and never asked any questions. Stayed here six months, sharp as a knife though. He disappeared one day. Every day, I expect to find his body somewhere in the woods. He had the longest range of anyone so far. He was so good. But, he disappeared."

"Did he..." Sean almost said the word *escape*, "leave?"

Mason shook his head. "No, he couldn't have. Not with that collar. It was during the week so I couldn't look much in the daytime. When I was finally able to look for him, I couldn't find him anywhere. Guessing an animal got to him or something. Made a grave for him all the same." Mason sniffled suddenly, and Sean noticed the thin slivers of snot trailing down from his nose onto his lips and chin. "I miss them all so much sometimes."

Mason threw down his post digger and looked at Sean as he said, "Y'know boy, I'm really glad I found you." Red started to ring around his eyes, and he smiled, appreciation gleaming in his cold eyes. "Each of my past boys had some imperfection. Three of them were constant runners. Two of them were ugly fat fucks. And the others were either zombies or too rebellious." He stopped and looked down at the hole he was halfway done with. "The last one was pretty damn good. Until he cheated on me."

Sean arched an eyebrow. "Cheated on you, sir? How? That doesn't..."— he noticed a fire grow in Mason's eyes as he stared at Sean then—"...make a lot of sense, sir."

"Doesn't it?" He aimed a gob of saliva at the hole again. "He fell in *love* with one of my *friends*." He practically spat the words *love* and *friends* at Sean. "They waited till I was at work. Then, they *kissed* and they *fucked* and they didn't give a *shit* about me." Mason's voice had been rising steadily so that now he was shaking, his hands clenched into fists, and his bald head turning as red as the rings around his eyes.

"I'm...I'm so sorry, sir," Sean offered, not at all apologetic.

"Don't be, boy. You'd never do that. If you don't love me yet, you will. I believe that." Mason wiped his nose on the back of his hairy forearm. "I killed them both."

"Huh?"

"I tied Eight up, rammed a knife into his stomach, split his ribs open. Then, I found Greg, smashed him up with a hammer, and pushed Eight's bloody fucking heart into his mouth, and that's what he finally choked to death on. I threw him into the woods. Better for the birds and the ants than a decent grave."

"Fuck!" Sean blurted, anger rising. "That's fucked up!" He covered his mouth as soon as he said it, dropping the post digger.

"Oh, is it, boy?" Mason said through his teeth, his own jaw clenching.

Sean took a step back but did not run.

Mason's face went livid. "You're overdue for a punishment, boy."

As Mason stepped toward Sean, Sean stepped back again and raised his hands defensively. "What do you mean, sir? I'm sorry, sir. I didn't mean to offend you, sir." His anger melted away, liquefying into a flood of terror. "Sir I meant that um...what they did was fucked up," he said, trying to double back on his words.

Sean felt the pressure of Mason's practiced fingers on the weak points of his neck, and, over the pain, he heard the growl in his master's voice as he was forced back toward the house: "Believe me, boy. This is for your own good. The sooner you learn..."

# 7

Sean stared in horror as Mason tied his hands and ankles to the corners of the leather-backed sawhorse. The edges of the wood pressed into his thighs and arms, and he knew he would have red indentations there after this punishment was over. His mind spiraled with what Mason was going to do to him. Was Mason just going to fuck him? Use a whip on him? The sex machine? Or would he just leave Sean bound here overnight?

Mason came around and held a leather strap with a red rubber ball in the center in front of Sean's face. "Open wide, boy." Sean clenched his jaw and shook his head, refusing even that complaisance, but Mason grabbed his neck, and, when he opened his mouth to cry out in pain, Mason shoved the ball gag inside, wrapping the straps around Sean's head and tying them tightly so Sean could not spit the ball back out. With a chain leash, he clipped Sean's collar to the front of the sawhorse, stopping even Sean's head from moving.

When Mason left the basement, his boots thudding up the stairs, Sean knew for sure that Mason planned on just leaving him overnight like this, a fleshy ornament in the cold damp of the basement. He huffed through his nose. *I can survive this. This'll be fine. It's just cold...and wet...and I'm hungry...but I'll be fine. I can just sleep through the night. I'm already lying down basically.*

Then, he heard footsteps on the stairs again, this time joined by faster, softer footsteps. He frowned, trying to make out what was happening. Had Mason brought a kid with him? The footsteps stopped behind Sean. All he could see was the stained and mildewy stone wall opposite the stairs. Mason patted Sean's back three times, the hard calluses slapping against Sean's sweaty flesh, and said, "Up, boy."

Sean rolled his eyes. He was so tightly bound that there was nothing he could raise, no matter how demanding Mason was: not his hips, not his legs, not even his head.

When he felt two furry objects land onto his back, he realized Mason hadn't been talking to him.

"Good boy," Mason said. Sean heard panting.

It was Max. Sean felt a hot and sharp object poke at his ass, and his whole body tensed, refusing entry. Now, he tried to move his hips, but all the struggle did was tighten the cords around his legs, numbing them. Spikes of terror shot through him, and he started screaming against the gag, straining his vocal cords, but only a slight *rrrrh!* coming out.

"Stay," Mason said. He came around into Sean's periphery, holding a needle. "Alright, boy, since this is a punishment, you can't be as drugged up as you were last week. So this," he added, pressing the needle into Sean's vein, "is a bit of cocaine to get your heart pumping again. I want you to *feel* this."

Sean's eyes widened. Mason stood there and stared into his eyes, as if waiting to see the change. Sean's heart pace quickened, and, within a minute, he felt like a veil had been lifted from his vision, like a haze had vanished. He started to struggle against his restraints again, trying at least to buck the dog off him. Mason smiled. Within another three minutes, Sean's heart was racing, the blood rushing to his cheeks, and his eyes darting around the room. He felt *everything*. His wrists and ankles throbbed where the restraints cut into his circulation. His head pounded with a splitting headache. The only heat he felt was where Max's paws were planted on the small of his back. His jaw felt sore from the gag that was holding his jaws open. His lips worked around the gag, trying to find a way to push it out of his mouth.

"There we go," Mason said, clearly content with the change he saw. He stood and faced the dog. "Alright, boy, go."

To Sean's surprise and horror, Max fucked him. The pointed flesh behind Sean drove home in one thrust—no lube, not even spit—and his insides felt like they were being torn with a blunt knife. Unlike the gangbang the week before, his senses were not a blur this time. The cocaine made his heart race, and his senses became hyper-alert. He felt *everything*. And *everything* hurt. Every single thrust was a bolt of lightning in his mind, a jolt of pain that shot up his spine and made his skull rattle.

"That's right," Mason said, his voice a soft and encouraging coo. "Good boy."

The voice, though soft, felt like nails in Sean's ears. And he wished for this to end. Each second, his mind yelled, *Stop!* but his prayers were left unanswered. He felt betrayed, not just by Mason, but by Max as well. The one being to show him kindness and affection was now turned against him, as much a sexual predator as Mason was now. Sean's one ally was just as evil. The pain was excruciating, and the shame of being put so low, the sex object for an animal, was almost worse, a part of this whole story he would probably never tell anyone, not even Janie or Devlin.

Mason stroked the back of Sean's neck, making Sean shiver with discomfort. "You're doing good, too, boy. I learned a few years ago to warm my boys up before they met the horses. Don't want Number Five to happen to anyone again." He chuckled to himself, and Sean imagined his eyes glinting.

Then, with another thrust, Sean felt an icicle of recognition pierce his mind. *Number Five...he's the one who died from the horses...He wasn't trampled.* Sean's eyes widened, and he found himself struggling wildly against the restraints again, moaning as loudly as he could against the gag and putting all of his weight into his movements. He didn't care if the restraints cut into his skin. He had to get out of this. And when he did, he would fight back. He would use the sawhorse or the postdigger from outside even. He *had* to fight Mason. This nightmare would never end unless he fought back, unless he *hurt* Mason, *killed* him.

With each of Max's thrusts, Sean envisioned using a knife to thrust into Mason's sides, and face, and groin, returning the pain Mason had inflicted on him the past several weeks.

After a hundred or so of these thrusts, Max finally stopped, spent, and leaned on Sean, panting, his knot tight and sore in Sean's ass. Just as exhausted, Sean wanted to yell and scream for the dog to get off, but the gag rendered that impossible. He found the energy to twist his hips, but again to no avail. He had to lie there, trying not to focus on that throbbing and pulsing inside him. He tried not to imagine what was inside him. But in trying *not* to imagine, he found himself inevitably picturing the pink flesh and the dog above him, content and ignorant of what had just happened.

He cried, not out of fear, but out of frustrated helplessness, his inability to do anything. He was helpless to get out of this situation or stop this from really happening again. He was at Mason's mercy, and a despairing side of his mind told him that he may as well get used to this. This would be his new life for now. But as soon as the thought surfaced, he forced it back down, refusing to acknowledge that possibility. Part of him wanted to fight, and part of him wanted to give in for now and plan. That struggle tore him. In front of him, clear as the stains on the wall, he saw his father kneeled before him. The man was laughing at him, hands on his knees. "Hey fag, you wanted to be a bitch, so here you go!" He laughed again at his own joke, and Sean's face flushed. "What's the matter? Cat got your tongue? Or is it a dog?" His dad practically fell over that time, and Sean closed his eyes, shutting out what he saw and what he heard. Tears fell down his cheeks and stung the corners of his lips where the ball gag's straps had cut him slightly. He felt so ashamed, more than he had his entire time here. He wanted to take a warm bath and clean himself of all this. He wanted to put on clothes and his nakedness from the world as he always had. He wanted to be a normal person again, not this broken toy for a dog.

"Down, boy," Mason said, and, with a sickening and excruciating *pop*, the dog pulled out, leaving Sean's anus to contract painfully.

Mason stooped down in front of Sean and unstrapped the ball gag, his blue eyes wet with sorrow and concern. But Sean could not meet his gaze. He felt like even Mason would judge him now, as if the whole incident had been his own fault, even though he knew that wasn't the case. "I'm sorry I had to do that, boy." He grasped Sean's cheeks between his callused hands and wiped away the tears. The action was so forceful that Sean flinched, expecting Mason to slap him or punch him. "I don't *like* to hurt you." And though Sean did not believe a word of this, he looked up into Mason's eyes and saw that *he* believed it.

"Then, why *did* you...sir?" Sean asked, trying his hardest to keep his voice level, though he knew it came out cracked, his throat sore from his straining.

"Because you needed to be punished, boy." He brushed a hand through Sean's hair. "And you've learned, haven't you?"

Sean gritted his teeth, although his face was now flushed with red. "Yes, sir."

Mason went on his knees and rubbed at Sean's face again, as if trying to massage it with sandpaper. "Boy...I...I think you're different from the others. I *know* you are."

Sean just looked at him, trying to read Mason's emotions but could not understand them.

"I know you're having a hard time adjusting. It's a whole new life, but I know you'll learn to love it. In just a few short weeks, you've already gotten better. You've only tried to run away once, and you've done such a good job with keeping the house clean. You're like the *perfect* boy."

"Th-thank you, sir," Sean managed, frowning.

"No, boy, you don't understand." Mason inched closer, so that his nose, pointed and oily, pressed against Sean's. "I *love* you, boy."

Sean stared back at the balding man in disbelief, in raw, angry disbelief. *He* loves *me?* Sean had every temptation to spit in the man's terrible eyes, but he could only guess how badly that would end. And right now, he didn't even have pride left to spend. *What could I say back to him? "I fucking hate you" would probably lead to more punishment... "Thank you" would be neutral but still not what he's wanting to hear...* "I...love you too, sir," he replied, feeling a lump in his throat. His vocal cords felt strained and sore from his attempts at screaming against the gag.

Mason laughed. "Good." He laughed again, wiping tears from his own eyes. "You are a good boy. You're such a good boy." He started untying Sean's restraints and shooed Max away, back upstairs.

Once Sean was completely free and standing, he rubbed his wrists, trying to return the blood flow. "Thank you, sir."

Mason stepped toward him and embraced him in a tight hug. With his face pressed into Sean's hair and then down to his neck, planting it with kisses, Mason whispered, "Tell me anything. I'll do anything to make you happy here, boy." He leaned back and grabbed Sean's shoulders, beaming. "What do you want? More toys? Certain foods? Books? Maybe you want your master to get you a nice leather pup hood?" Mason smiled with each suggestion as if each were a clever new idea that made him realize how good a guy he really was.

Sean was tempted to shake his head. *How about some freedom? Or maybe just a gun so I can put some bullets in you?* he thought. Then, he realized that this was his chance. "Well...there is something I'd like, sir..."

Mason's smile spread, forming wrinkles across his leathery face. "Yes! Yes! Anything!" His word sprayed spittle onto Sean's face, and Sean tried to pretend he hadn't.

"Well, sir..." He knew he had to be careful here. If he came across as too eager, Mason would worry that Sean was trying to "cheat" on him. "I kinda liked that party from that one weekend..."

"You did?" Mason said, shaking Sean's shoulders. "Well, that's easy! I can schedule another one whenever you want."

Sean shook his head, wincing, both at the direction Mason's mind immediately went toward and the pain that was starting to flare in his rectum. "Um, no, sir. I liked it more...near the end...when there were just two of you left. Having a group of guys around is fun, but I like...just having two cocks to work...sir."

"Ah," Mason said, raising his eyebrows and still smiling. "Well, I can arrange that. Anyone in particular you want to come?"

This time, Mason's eyes seemed to be searching Sean's, as if looking for anything that might be affection for someone besides him. "Well, a lot of them seemed rude to you, sir. And talked about you when you walked out of the room." Mason's face flushed, and his smile faded. "The only one who didn't laugh along—I think that was the guy who was leaning against the wall during dinner. Do you remember him, sir?"

Mason nodded. "Oh sure, that's Dustin. So...you want him because...?"

"Because he and you are *men*, sir. The others were just..."—he almost said dogs—"pigs."

Mason's smile returned. "Damn right, boy. Alright, if that's what my boy wants, he'll have it. Might have him over a few weekends in a row then." He laughed. "He's got a good cock, doesn't he? And my faggot boy likes those cocks in him, too, huh?" He didn't wait for a response. "I'll let him know. When he's free, I'll get him to come down." He ruffled Sean's hair again. "You're such a *good* boy."

As Mason left the basement, leaving Sean there to recover, Sean watched him leave, eyes boring into his plain gray t-shirt, wishing his gaze could shoot fire into that spine. He scanned the room one last time before following Mason, wishing something here could be used as a weapon. But he knew that anything that could be used had probably been tried by one of the other boys. He had to think outside the box, and he didn't have many chances. For now, he had to keep his head low.

·    ·    ·    ·    ·    ·    ·

Sean worked patiently for the next several days, though he tried not to move around too much and give his ass time to heal. Even walking seemed to open the tears there. It wasn't until the next Thursday when Dustin was finally able to come over one night. By this time, Sean could at least walk normally again. Mason had gone over the rules with Sean, mostly warning him not to try any funny business about cheating on him or setting up outside meetings. And Sean continued to reassure Mason that he only had an interest in doing this because of the feeling of a threesome. Being the love-crazed psychopath that he was, Mason believed it.

Sean had it all planned. He would try to get Mason on his ass and Dustin in his mouth. That way, Mason would finish well before Dustin, and he would leave Sean and Dustin alone for a while. If there's one thing Sean had noticed about Mason—besides his primitive cravings for dominance— it was that when he was done, he was *done*. And Sean planned to use that to his advantage.

When Dustin came through the front door that night, Sean tried to hide a smile but failed. As soon as Mason turned his back, Dustin winked at him, and Sean's heart leaped. This guy could really be his chance out of here. Dustin would be his way out. Now that even Max had even betrayed him, the dog he now wanted nothing to do with, Dustin was his only hope of freedom, of comfort, of being a normal person again.

They ate dinner around the TV, and Sean served them, rubbing Mason's feet as he chatted with Dustin about sports, a subject that might as well have been French to Sean. They watched football, and Sean would have been shaking with anticipation if it weren't for the drugs keeping him down. Even with them working through his system though, he still felt as if time were going faster. Dinner ended. He picked up the dishes. Then, Mason called him into the living room, where he and Dustin were already naked, cocks standing at attention. Mason wiggled a finger, urging Sean toward them. He obeyed with a smile—not because he was eager to taste, but because he longed to get Mason off as quickly as possible.

After a few minutes of sucking each cock, taking each one deep in his throat before moving to the next, Mason led them upstairs, and Sean's heart pounded faster. That meant Mason had to be getting closer, if he was taking them upstairs already. Sean assumed the position once he was on the bed: on his hands and knees, back arched, nose pressed against Dustin's cock, his ass aimed toward Mason's. For the first time in his weeks here, he felt the slightest bit in control.

"How about it, boy?" Mason said, leaning over and ruffling Sean's hair like he was now not just a sex object but a dog as well. "You want me to go get the restraints for you?"

Sean shook his head. "No, sir. I...want you two to be able to throw me in whatever positions you want."

Mason's eyes glimmered, but Dustin winced visibly at the subservience. But, regardless of any reservations Dustin may have had, he fucked as eagerly as Mason. Sean was careful to not try too hard on Dustin's cock, limiting his use of tongue and not letting Dustin fuck his face too deeply. The drugs helped, and he was thankful that he had those. Addicted or not, he was able to not get caught up in the moment, to not feel, just think. Mason came within ten minutes, growling with each wave of orgasm that hit him. In that moment, Sean imagined him as a bulldog: strong, gruff, yet still simple-minded.

Mason heaved a long sigh as he put his jeans back on, letting his stomach hang out a little over the waistband. Then, Sean heard the words he had worked so hard to get Mason to say: "Alright boys, I'm gonna go watch some TV downstairs. Call if you need me."

Sean stopped sucking and listened. The footsteps pounded down the stairs, and he heard the TV turn back on. And then, Sean was finally alone with Dustin. Sitting up, his eyes met Dustin's smile. He took a deep breath.

# 8

Looking up at Dustin, Sean saw two things: a god and a human. On one hand, Sean knew that Dustin might be his only salvation from this personal hell, might be the one who could get him out of here and back into the real world. *Why haven't the cops found me yet? Or the FBI? Or someone?* Dustin's bare skin shone in the light from the ceiling, and the sweat glistened. Sure, he wasn't Adonis—perfection in flesh bound—but he very well could have been Zeus for his toned, middle-aged body. On the other hand, Dustin's cock was hard and throbbing, and Sean saw the lust in his eyes, cold and predatory. Dustin *had* to be better than Mason. All Sean had to do was find one normal person, and if Dustin could even get him away from Mason, that'd be a chance at finding a normal person. The trick would be to get Dustin to trust him. What Sean hadn't anticipated, however, was Dustin's utter fear of Mason.

Dustin laughed. "I appreciate that you feel you need me, Sean." The use of his real name—instead of "boy"—sent the most grateful of shivers down his spine. "But I couldn't take you away from here for even a day. You're hot as hell, and Mason's a lucky one to have found you." *More like "kidnapped,"* Sean thought. "But I'd be the craziest man alive to try to take a boy away from Mason. He killed the last guy who tried to do that."

Sean's eyes widened. *You know he killed a guy, and you're just...content with that? Don't have even the instinct to call the cops on him?* "Um..." Sean started, face flushing and unsure how to proceed. "I just...I don't...I don't *like* it here, sir."

Dustin shook his head. "You don't have to call me that, especially while *he's* not around." He put his hands on Sean's shoulders and rocked his hips forward, rubbing his wet cocktip around Sean's face, leaving a sticky trail of precum from Sean's nose down around to his chin. "Well, maybe I'll talk to Mason and see what I can do. He's not that bad when you get to know him.

He's just a bit possessive. He trusts me more than the others, and he knows I'll back off if he starts baring his teeth. He *knows* I'm terrified of him."

"Thank y—" Sean started, but, once he opened his mouth, Dustin shoved his cock into Sean's throat, balls pressing against Sean's chin.

"You're welcome, Sean. Now finish me off before we go downstairs. He'll be suspicious if we walk down there with me still having a hard-on."

But even as he thrust, his fingers rubbed down Sean's back, the warmest of touches. Even as fucked-up as this all was, Sean knew these touches were probably some of the most comforting moments of connection he would be feeling until he got out of here.

*That's what I'll do,* Sean thought. *I just gotta break Dustin's defenses down a bit, wear down Mason's, too, and then this will all work out. It will just take some time, that's all.* This reasoning softened his resolve, gave him confidence. And when Dustin finally came, Sean didn't feel exhausted; he felt invigorated, like Dustin and he shared a special secret, and that secret was a plan, a way out. The collar around his neck somehow didn't feel as tight.

As they made their way downstairs, Dustin called to Mason. "Hey Mason, you've been keeping your boy in good shape, I see."

"Damn right!" was Mason's call back.

Dustin grabbed a beer from the coffee table and sat down beside Mason, sighing heavily and sprawling out as if to show off his saliva-coated cock. Sean sat down beside the couch and stared blankly at the television while the others sat in their afterglow.

It was Mason who broke the silence. "Hey Dusty."

"Hm?" Dustin said, bringing the beer up to his lips.

"I know you like my little boy toy, and I know you won't ever fuck up as bad as Tommy did." Sean saw Dustin flinch. "But I'm going out of town in a couple of weeks—for a week—and maybe you could stay here and watch the boy? Make sure he *stays* in good use?" Mason turned to look at Dustin now, and Sean knew all of a sudden that Mason was testing him.

"Sure," Dustin said, shrugging. "If you need me to, I will. Not sure I'll use him as much as you probably think I will. But I can make sure the boy doesn't starve to death or anything." He faced Mason. "And I'll still have to go to work, so I'll only really be here on nights. That fine with you?"

73

Mason nodded and smiled. "Yeah, fine with me. He's easy to take care of. Just be careful." He took another swig of his Budweiser, a thin stream of the beer trickling out of the corner of his mouth and down his chin.

Dustin nodded in return, and Sean wondered at the turn of phrase. As Sean sat there, he stared blankly at the screen, his eyes looking through the football players and the cheering fans. Trying to distract himself so as not to betray his interest in Dustin, he tried to envision the last time he had sat down at a football game. It had been one of the games during his freshman year. The Southern Tennessee Possums—yes, their mascot was typical roadkill—had lost for only the hundredth time, yet the students in the stands had cheered: the Possums had scored three touchdowns, an impressive record apparently. With the noise of the cheers, the smells of sweat and greasy food, Sean had promised to never go to another game. Now, he wondered if he'd ever have even the chance to see one again. He imagined both Devlin and Janie sitting there in the stands, cheering on a losing team. For some reason, his vision had them holding hands, which made little sense, considering Devlin's general aversion to pussy.

When the game ended, Dustin got up, shook hands with Mason, ruffled Sean's hair, and left, without saying a word. Once the door was shut, Sean stood up and went upstairs to get another dose of the benzos, his nerves starting to get to him again. He had considered ways to slowly ease himself off the drugs, still emptying a syringeful into the mattress or something to hide the fact from Mason. But even with his full strength and senses, he was not too confident that he would be able to do anything at all. At least, the drugs kept his nerves down for the most part, made him more objective with his thoughts and less panicked.

As he pressed down on the top of the syringe, feeling that warmth fill his vein, he thought back to Janie and Devlin. *If I get out of here, I promise I'll treat them better,* he thought. *I'll spend more time with Janie, and I'll let Dev set me up with dates like he's always wanted to.* A part of him hoped that these kinds of promises would magically send the hand of God down to the house, pop off his collar, and open the front door. But no such divine intervention came.

Mason called from downstairs, "Hey boy, make sure you shower. I'm gonna wanna fuck you again before I go to bed."

"Yes, sir!" he yelled back.

With a low whine in his throat, he grasped at the collar again, pulling on it, trying to wedge his fingers between it and his skin, but it was far too tight. It had not loosened at all since it had been placed on him that first night. He had come here for a good lay. Now, he found himself regretting every sexual urge he had ever felt. He missed his bed. He missed his apartment. He missed his friends and school and his car. He missed his dad.

Under the shower's soap and steam, he cried, his temple pressed against the tiled wall.

•   •   •   •   •   •   •

On the day that Mason was supposed to leave and Dustin was to come over, Mason called Sean into his bedroom. Dutifully, Sean entered and stared at his master, who was dressed in a full suit, black blazer, slacks, and all. "Hey boy, I need to talk to you about something."

"Yes sir," Sean started, "I know not to 'try anything' with the other guy. I have no interest in him other than him being a friend of my master's."

Mason stopped packing clothes, turned, and smiled at Sean. "Good boy. That's not what I wanted to talk to you about, though."

Sean raised an eyebrow. "What is it, sir?"

As Mason went back to packing some clothes, Sean looked around the room. He had been in here a few times since this nightmare had started, often looking for sharp implements or a gun or just some object he could use to facilitate his escape, but no such object could be found. There was a queen-sized bed in the center, two dressers, a desk where Mason kept a lot of his accounting paperwork for his "freelance handyman" work, and a nightstand with a lamp and a few football cards. The closet was full of leather jackets, harnesses, and loafers, as if the man solely wore leather—though Sean had only seen him in full leather garb three times.

Mason threw a few pairs of jockstraps into the suitcase, and Sean wondered what other activities Mason had planned at this business trip. Mason started, "Well, I got a few things while I was in town yesterday. Picked up some lumber, some food for you this week, an ax so you can chop us some firewood this winter...and I got you a present." He paused as if wanting Sean to respond.

Clearing his throat, Sean said, "Yes, sir?" He held his hands behind his back, picking at his fingernails nervously.

Mason walked over to one of his dressers, opened a drawer, and pulled out what looked like a ring box, small, black, and immaculate. He walked back over to Sean and held the box out to him. "For you, boy."

Sean grabbed the box, trying not to look into Mason's expectant eyes. When he opened the box, he saw a glimmer within. His first thought—and fear—was that it was a ring and that for some fucked-up reason, Mason might be proposing to him. But what he saw was only a slight comfort. It was a silver dog tag, in the shape of a bone. On its face was a name with small text in all caps beneath it. Sean read aloud, "Bo...Property of Bill Mason." On the back of the tag was the house address.

When Sean looked up, Mason appeared as if he were about to cry tears of joy. "Well? What do you think, boy? You like it?"

"I...um..." Sean started, shaking his head and looking back down at the tag. He repeated the name, "Bo..." He found himself thinking back to when Mason had Max rape him. Now, Sean was to be as much an object of sex as Max clearly was. The flashback shot through his heart and left him breathless. *The animal that now I am...* Sean thought bitterly, parodying a philosophy text from college.

"Yes," Mason said, nodding his head vigorously as he admired Sean holding the tag in his fingers. "That's your new name. Do you like it?"

The other boys had not been "good" enough for Mason. A mixture of failed escape attempts, lack of caution, and "cheating" had led to their deaths. Sean had to outlast them. If he was clever, he could survive this. "I love it, sir. Thank you."

"Good, now it's time to complete the ceremony, wouldn't you say?" Mason moved closer, grabbing the tag, and fixing it to Sean's collar. "Good boy, Bo." He ruffled Sean's hair, and Sean felt an urge to growl and bite Mason's fingers. Mason walked back to his suitcase and closed it. Just as he zipped it, they heard a knock at the door. Dustin. "Oh, before I forget, Bo, your disappearance from school has got some police trying to find you. So, make sure that you stay inside while I'm gone and don't talk to any policemen if they come by, alright?"

Sean frowned but nodded and said, "Yes, sir. Of course, sir." His heart leaped. *They* are *trying to find me. Maybe, there's a chance then. I just have to stay alive long enough for them to get here.* He made sure not to let Mason see how excited the prospect made him.

"I don't want to lose my perfect little Bo now that I've found him." He grabbed Sean's neck then and pulled him close, pressing his whiskered lips against Sean's, forcing his tongue—a dry slab of flesh that tasted of cheap whiskey and even cheaper tobacco—to wrap around Sean's. It took all of Sean's energy not to gag, but he managed to pull away.

"I should probably get the door, sir. I don't want to make your...guest wait."

"Good Bo. Send him in." Mason gave him a playful slap on the ass as Sean walked out.

When Sean opened the door, Dustin was standing there with a suitcase of his own, though notably smaller than Mason's. "Here, boy," Dustin said, handing Sean the case with a sly and knowing wink.

"Thank you, sir," Sean replied, taking the case and bringing it toward Mason's room where Dustin would be sleeping. "Your friend is here, sir," Sean called as he walked toward Mason.

Mason came out with the suitcase, patted Sean on the head, gave a quick "Goody boy," shook hands with Dustin, and was out the door. And like a class full of kids when a substitute walks in, Sean smiled, knowing the rules of the game had changed. He felt freer already. He walked to the window and watched the headlights of the Ford Ranger disappear into the woods. With a frown, he noted that his Dodge Intrepid was gone entirely. It had sat in the driveway this whole time, wet leaves and fallen sticks clinging to its roof for weeks. But now, it was gone. Maybe Mason had driven it into the woods? Or maybe sold it to a dealer in town? Regardless of what had been done with it, however, there was nothing he could do about it now. He realized he would probably never see that car again.

"He's gone..." Sean said, loud enough for Dustin to hear.

"Good, now let's get you out of here." Together, they worked on grabbing Sean's box from downstairs. Next on the agenda was to get the collar off. Within minutes, they were heading down the road, past the barn and the cemetery, across the river, and back to the main highway.

This was what Sean envisioned happening when he heard Mason's car fade out into the distance, the wind replacing the whir of his engine. But after announcing Mason's exit, all he heard was the sound of Dustin's belt being undone. Sean's smile faltered. He knew, then, it was going to be another long night.

# 9

Sean learned quickly that Dustin was a different kind of master than Mason. Even as a college student, Sean had thought there was only one type of psychopath, the grinning sadist who delighted in people's misfortune—kind of your typical crime TV show serial killer. But as Sean was learning, there were two: the kind that doesn't know that what they are doing is wrong—like Mason—and the kind that *delights* in knowing that what they are doing is wrong—like Dustin.

Dustin saw Sean as a person, rather than as a dog or an object. But that is part of what made him so dangerous. He felt no remorse when he pulled strips of white-and-green striped nylon cord out of his black bag and hog-tied Sean on top of the coffee table, his chin resting on the rough edge and his balls squished under him. He felt no sorrow when he took out a crop, a leather-covered handle with four leather cords about three feet in length protruding from it, and whipped it across Sean's back, flaying his skin and raising welts within seconds. Each stroke brought out cries of pain from Sean as he arched his back, and each cry brought a smile to Dustin's lips.

That first time, Sean did not last more than ten strokes before passing out. Of course, the drugs had kept him close to that unconscious state anyway. The pain just eased him along. When he came to, maybe an hour later, he was no longer bound, but his ass was sore. Feeling along it with a finger, he felt Dustin's cum there. He had been fucked while he was out. Inspecting himself, he saw his body was covered in raised welts and bruises. Thin red lines indicated where his skin had been slashed open by the crop, and each cut stung. "What the fuck," Sean said, touching his skin softly, tracing over his elevated flesh. Sean was well aware that not even sadists in the BDSM community beat you enough to where you bled like this.

He heard the water of the shower running; Dustin must have been cleaning up after raping him. Sean approached the window overlooking the front yard, his bare feet stepping carefully across the carpet. Only Dustin's white Toyota Camry in the driveway. If this pain that covered his body was what he had to look forward to this week, Sean almost preferred Mason. He thought that if Mason would come back, he would work harder to be a "good boy." He would not even think of escaping. Maybe that kind of good behavior would give him more freedom, at least from this pain. In college, he had always hated the phrase "out of the frying pan and into the fire." He always claimed it was an overused cliché—his mom had used it often enough. But now, looking down at where the crop had flayed him, he could think of no better phrase.

Dustin had lied to him, and that was probably the worst part of this whole scenario. For weeks, he had seen Dustin as this glowing hope for escape, that maybe there was a way out, after all. And Dustin had been content leading him on. The man was a true sadist, reveling in the misery that false hope had given Sean. Desperate for any chance, Sean had leaped at the hope. He had practically begged Dustin to stay and watch over him. More and more, he was regretting that decision.

A year ago, he thought he was a submissive with few limits, a bottomless hole eagerly taking whatever dick was offered to it. He had even worked around his usual limits for the right guy. But now, every hard limit had been violated in the most ruthless ways by Mason, Dustin, and the others from the gang-rape. He had little integrity left from it all, and his experiences had left him broken on the inside, not sure if he could ever trust a guy again, assuming he ever did make it out of this situation, a possibility he was believing possible less and less with each passing day, if not every hour. Despite his prior appetites, his cock hadn't been hard since that first week. He did not find pleasure in even the most basic of sex, not that Mason or Dustin ever really did anything basic. For the first time in years, Sean wondered if he would ever have sexual desire again. He felt unclean. He felt corrupted. And, worst of all, he felt subhuman, unworthy of another loving gaze.

Out of the corner of his eye, he saw his dad, bent over at the waist, hands on his knees, laughing at him. The man seemed a permanent fixture there. Sean was not sure if it was a side effect of the drugs or his own traumatized mind, but nevertheless, everywhere he went, his old man lingered in his peripheral sights, mocking his every move and reveling in his fate. In his few moments of privacy, such as being in the shower or doing lawn work, he found himself talking to his dad, begging him to stop, but all the same, his dad was the only familiar company. Sean knew how to handle *that* abuse.

"Save me," he whispered, his eyes still focusing on the outdoors, not daring to look at his dad for fear the old man would disappear. His eyes scanned the doghouse, wishing even Max could come in and rescue him. The dog was comfort in some ways, but in others, Sean knew the terror Mason had raised, the beast Mason had trained Max to be. Seeing how bad Dustin was, Sean was starting to forgive Max, realizing that the dog's issues were taught, not instinctive. And even as he knew his father's figure could sense these embarrassing memories, Sean begged. "Please, Dad, just this one time. I'll do whatever it takes, whatever you want. Just help me."

"Sure," the husky voice responded, and Sean's eyes widened. He was tempted to turn. "I'm going to need you to find some rope first."

"Dad? Rope?" He finally turned, and his father was gone.

His mind replayed the words before continuing them: *I'm going to need you to find some rope first.* His father laughed. *Then attach it to a ceiling fan or hook or something, get on a chair, tie the other end around your neck and JUMP!* The man hooted again, the laugh seeming to echo across the room.

Sean wiped his red-rimmed eyes and eased his way upstairs, careful with each step not to let his footfalls be audible to Dustin in the bathroom. He could barely make out the sounds of Dustin humming in the shower. It was soft, and Sean couldn't tell what it was, but it was there.

Finally upstairs, Sean took comfort in the sight of the syringe. He plunged the needle into his arm with one practiced hand and sighed when he expelled its contents into his vein. Numbness. At this point, covered in blood from the cuts and sweat that stung, feeling nothing was bliss. He absently wondered if the marks would scar. He wondered what Mason would do, think, or say when he saw Sean like this. Would he think Sean probably deserved it? Would he lash out at Dustin? Or, even worse, would he not even notice?

Over the next few days, things fell into a terrifying rhythm. Dustin had work, and when he returned, he would tie Sean, whip him till he fell unconscious, shower, and leave Sean to do what he wished. Generally, Dustin cooked for himself, but, when in the same room as Sean, he tried to make pleasant conversation. Each time, he asked Sean about what life was like *before* Mason. The conversations almost made Sean like Dustin. In this way, Dustin was both alluring and terrifying. When not wielding the lash, Dustin seemed genuinely interested in Sean's life and his very humanity, treating Sean like a person.

With each conversation, Sean spoke, a small smile hanging on his face. During one dinner together, he thought, *This is ridiculous. I'm being grateful that I'm not being treated like a sex object for the first time since I left home...No...I'd rather be a sex object than this. At least with Mason, he doesn't delight in my pain. He only hurts me when he thinks I deserve it. At least I have some control there. This bastard just enjoys hurting me.* Then, he experienced another first that almost brought him to tears in the middle of his conversation with Dustin, a thought that chilled him to his core: *I miss Mason.*

His mind swung from one place to another. He would go from hating Mason for ever starting this whole mess, to loathing Dustin for betraying him, to despising even himself for giving Dustin this much power. He cursed Mason for not giving him enough drugs, the benzos that made the pain at least tolerable. He felt as if he needed double the dose to handle the pain Dustin was pleased to dish out, but instead, Sean had to ration his doses, hoping that Mason would return on time.

There came one day when Sean considered writing a will, a letter for Mason to discover in case he died in Dustin's care. He imagined some of the things he would say: "Sir, please leave my body in my car for my family to find near the school or something." "Please don't bury me in the graveyard with the other boys." "Sir...don't let Dustin get away with this."

He was furious—with Mason, Dustin, Max, and himself. Some days— most of the days with Dustin so far—he felt like all of this was his own fault, as if, maybe, by doing a better job listening to Mason, he would not have had the terrible and violent strings of rape and abuse. In his drug-addled mind, this was completely rational. His new world revolved around the fundamentals of cause and effect. If he was good and obedient, he would be rewarded. If he was bad and rebellious, he would be punished. And he was only coming to terms with that now, as Dustin was showing him that even good behavior could come with a beating.

*I miss Mason.*

. . . . . . .

Wednesday, Sean was tied down again, thin, wiry ropes holding his hands and arms behind his back and his ankles bound together. A piss- and sweat-stained pair of white briefs had been forced into his mouth gagging him. This time, when Dustin used the whip on him, it felt sharper, opening up each cut from the days before and making them bleed afresh. It was after the fifth stroke when they heard Max barking outside, the dog finally acting as a herald of hope.

Dustin stopped what he was doing, approached the window, stretched the blinds with two fingers, and looked out. Sean breathed through his nose and tried to clear his mind, hoping for consciousness to leave him sooner rather than later.

"Oh, shit," Dustin said.

Sean opened his eyes hazily to see what Dustin was freaking out about, but from his position sitting on the carpet in front of the TV, he could not see through the window.

Interpreting Sean's dazed look as confusion, Dustin explained, "It's the cops. They've found us." He looked back in the direction of the window. "They're coming up the road."

Sean's heart started to throb hopefully. He moaned against the gag, but his mouth was dry, the underwear having soaked up all the moisture in his mouth.

At the sound, Dustin rushed to pull off his socks and force them into Sean's mouth too. "Fuck no. Not one sound out of you, got it? You let them know you're here, and I will gut you before the cop even lays a finger on you, understand? Not one. Damn. Sound." He looked around. "Um, now where to hide you..."

Max's barking was louder now.

"How about in the kitchen..." He rushed past Sean and across the hallway to the tiled kitchen. Within seconds, he was calling back, half to himself and half to Sean, as he strode back, "Yeah, that'll do." He grabbed onto the first thing he could, Sean's hair, and pulled, dragging him across the carpeted hallway toward the kitchen. Sean tried to scream, but the underwear and socks in his mouth cut off all sound completely, so he had to struggle to hear the vibration even in his own ears. The pain was immense, and he was bound too tightly to do anything about it. Finally, his ass bumped over the metal trim piece separating the hallway from the kitchen, landing hard on the tile. Dustin let go of his hair. *He's going to shove me in the oven,* Sean thought with terror. *He's going to cook me alive to hide the evidence.*

They heard the doorbell, followed by three heavy knocks.

"Shit," Dustin said, louder. He swung a cabinet door open from beneath the counter. There were a few Tupperware bowls on the cabinet bottom, but otherwise it was empty. "Perfect."

Sean's eyes went wild with fright, shaking his head, even as Dustin grabbed him by his bindings and flung him into the space, his head slamming into the back wall within. Stars flooded his vision. Dustin leaned forward into the doorway of the cabinet. "Not one goddamn word. Or it'll be your last." He slammed the cabinet door, ignoring Sean's knee which had been pressed against the doorway, and they both heard the cracking sound. For Sean, the pain was an instant firework that shot up his leg and spine. But again, he could make no sound. As Dustin forced Sean's shattered knee through the cabinet, Sean saw a smile flick across his face as the door was closed properly.

Sean struggled to stay conscious now, for there was hope the officer would find him, save him, and take him back. Above the splintering fire that was spreading through his leg and the rawness of his scalp, he felt hope.

He heard knocking continue once more before Dustin must have opened it. With the house being as open as it was, Sean did not struggle too much in hearing the words between Dustin and the officer.

"Oh, hello, officer, sorry I was downstairs when you knocked."

"No worries, sir." The officer's voice sounded softer than Dustin's. Probably a younger guy. "Are you John Mason?"

"John? Oh no. I'm here dogsitting for him while he's away for a work trip."

"Oh, is that so? When is he expected to be back?"

"Sometime this weekend. That's all he's told me."

"Alright." There was a pause. "And your name?"

"Oh, my name's Dustin Garner."

"Dustin Garner? Are you from around here?"

"No sir, I leave about a couple hours away, over in Athens."

"Athens, huh? Well, have you heard about the missing boy Sean Wolfe?"

Another pause. Sean could hear his heartbeat in his ears. "Oh yeah, seen him on the TV and all. Probably just ran away though or something. Kid like that in a backwater college. Didn't his father just die, too?"

"Yes, sir. That's correct. Poor kid. But he probably didn't run away. Anyhow, we have some camera footage showing which way out of the city he took, so we've been asking people in a thirty-mile radius if they've heard anything. Do you think you or Mr. Mason could help us out at all?"

Another pause. "Oh, I don't know. I can probably ask him when he gets back if you'd like. I haven't heard anything else besides what I've been seeing on the TV though. It's all quiet out here anyway. Just me and the dog."

"That's fine. Uh, mind if I have a look around?"

"Sure! By all means, help yourself, officer."

Sean could hear them go upstairs, and he could no longer hear what they were saying, just the sounds of the officer's shoes thudding on the stairs. Sean tried to slow his breathing and focus on listening, but it was silent. After a few minutes, Sean started to wonder if Dustin had killed the officer. But then, he heard their descent down the stairs again. He breathed a sigh of relief through his nose, and the pain in his leg grew again.

"—and down here we have the bathroom, John's room, and the kitchen."

"Alright."

Sean heard a few of the doors open and close, as if the officer were giving each one a cursory glance more as a formality than as a serious investigation. Sean found himself internally screaming at the officer, *Why didn't you check the basement with the boxes of our stuff? Or see all the fucked up equipment in the closet in Mason's room? Where did Dustin hide the whip he was beating me with just ten minutes ago? I'm right here, dammit!*

Then, they stepped into the kitchen. Through a small crack between the cabinet door and the doorway, light became shadow as a figure leaned against the doorway. "See? Nothing here, officer." It was Dustin. He was standing in front of the cabinet.

"Sure looks like it," the officer said. Sean was sure of it now: the guy had to be in his late twenties or early thirties. Sean heard the officer open the pantry door, a few cabinets, even the fridge.

"You can grab one of those Buds if you'd like, officer."

"Nah thanks. I'm on the clock and all."

Sean was sorely tempted to bang his head on the cabinet door and reveal his location, but fear stopped him. Sean imagined Dustin taking a fork and stabbing Sean in the eye with it or taking the toaster and bashing the officer's head in. Dustin, in some ways, was even crazier than Mason, and that level of unpredictability was horrifying. And in Sean's current state, he was in no position to resist or fight back.

Through the door, Sean heard the officer say, "Well, I guess I will leave you alone. But if you hear anything, give us a call. And tell Mr. Mason to let us know when he gets back so we can ask him a few questions, too, alright?"

The shadow moved as Dustin followed the officer out of the kitchen. "Oh of course, officer. I will let him know next time I hear from him. Yes, sir."

"Please do. Thank you kindly."

"No, thank you, officer!"

The door closed, and Max was barking again. The officer was gone.

Dustin grabbed the cord holding Sean's legs together and pulled him out of the cabinet with one hand, the rope cutting into his skin all over and causing his shattered knee to explode in pain. "Very good, Sean," Dustin said, laughing to himself. He pulled the gags out of Sean's mouth and worked on undoing the knots in the rope himself. "As reward, I'll let you go for the day. No more crop today." He laughed again. "That idiot cop almost found us out, huh?"

Sean nodded shakily, rubbing his wrists and ankles to get circulation flowing again.

"Alright, I'm going to hit the shower. When I get out, we'll start thinking about what's for dinner, yeah?"

Sean nodded again, and Dustin left the kitchen, pulling off his shirt as he did.

Once Sean heard the sound of running water, Dustin called back, "Mason would be proud of you, you know? He really doesn't deserve you, Sean. You're better than him."

*Yeah fucking right,* Sean thought. *If you really thought I was that special, you'd help me get out of here...Or no, maybe you do think I'm that special, and that's just even more reason to fuck with me. Me, the unwilling canvas to your leather-tongued brush.* He shivered but did not reply to Dustin.

Once Sean had removed all the bindings, he grabbed onto a counter edge, pushed himself up to a mostly standing position, and stretched everything but the leg with the ruined knee, which was now purple and swollen. Each movement pulled on the cuts, but his muscles felt instant relief.

"What's the matter, boy?" Sean's father said, looming ever in the corner of his eye. "You look like you picked a fight with a lawnmower...and lost!" The man was keeled over laughing again, as loud and exaggerated as he was in life.

"Shut up," Sean replied. "At least I've survived."

The man stopped laughing. Sean could see the silhouette move closer, until the old man's whiskey- and tobacco-tainted stench breathed into his ear, Mason-like, "At least I lived, *boy.*"

Then, he was gone.

Sean limped to the sink, filled a styrofoam cup with water, and chugged it down, appreciating the cool moisture in his mouth, rinsing out the sweat and piss of Dustin's old underwear. His father's words kept ringing in his ears. "At least I've *lived.*" It was a statement Sean's dad had made countless times when Sean was growing up. When sharing childhood stories with philosophy colleagues, Sean had often restated his dad simply by saying, "He used to think the ends *always* justified the means. The possession of the experience mattered more than the experience itself." It made for fun banter. But hearing these words now, from his ghost father, Sean knew he was right. *I'm surviving but not exactly living.* He realized he had been trying to bargain with all the powers in his life now: his dad, Mason, Dustin, even God. But none of those could or would let him out of this.

On his pained stagger to the stairs, he heard Dustin singing in the shower, some 90s rock tune he recognized. It was a song his father had always played in the car. Sean found himself humming along but not remembering the words. He turned his head and saw on the coffee table Dustin's cellphone. He had left it there while he went to take his shower. Looking back to make sure Dustin was still in the bathroom, door closed, Sean limped over to the table and grabbed the cellphone.

*Please don't be locked...Please don't be locked.* He pressed the Power button. The screen lit up. It wasn't locked. His thumb flicked the icon for Messages. A few names flashed into his vision: James, Derek, Mason, Cheryl...But he flicked the Plus icon for a new message. In the contact slot, he typed in Janie's number, one of the few phone numbers he had memorized completely.

*Sean 419 chickasaw rd get cops dont txt back.* As soon as he pressed SEND, he deleted the conversation, turned off the display, and made his way back to the stairs, the whole process taking a little less than a minute, but the suddenness burning through his leg. He did not stop till he was back in his room and on his bed. The shower was still running down below, but his heart was thudding in his chest.

He had done it. He had sent a text to the world outside.

He injected another dose into his arm and laid back against his pillow, looking up at the ceiling and melting into the numbness. There was hope. He laughed softly. "Take *that*, old man." His father was silent.

After a few minutes, the shower downstairs stopped running. Sean's smile faded, and fear replaced his joy. What if Janie had texted back anyway? What if Dustin saw fingerprints that weren't his on the phone screen? What if Sean hadn't closed the Messages app? There were so many possibilities for this to have gone wrong, and each one sent more spikes of fear through him.

When Dustin got out of the shower, Sean stayed up in his room, too terrified now to come down at all. He waited, half-expecting Dustin to call out "What the fuck did you do?" or, like some bear out of a fairy tale, "Who's been touching *my* phone?" But Dustin never said a word, at least not audibly.

The night went on. Dinner was like what it was with Mason. Sean was responsible for cooking, and, when he was done, they ate in front of the TV. However, unlike Mason, Dustin insisted that Sean sit beside him on the couch rather than in front of it. Often, during the TV programs, Dustin would reach between Sean's bare legs and squeeze his balls roughly, pulling them until Sean groaned in pain. Sean had learned the first night with Dustin not to try to move away. His balls still felt a little bruised from that. But as long as he was complacent, Dustin was comparatively gentle. During the shows, Dustin started conversation, asking about what Sean did with the dinner, as if genuinely interested in Sean's limited culinary knowledge, but Sean obliged, delighted to have any kind of conversation really, no matter how superficial it was. The whole time, Sean expected Dustin to flash that wicked grin and say something like, "I saw your message. I had to have your friend killed, Sean. I hope you don't mind." But Dustin did nothing of the sort.

Then, it was time for bed. If Dustin knew something was up, he did not give Sean any clue that he knew. Lying in in bed again, Sean wondered how this would go down. He imagined thirty cops busting through the front door, pinning Dustin to the ground, and rescuing Sean in an ambulance. Or maybe a sniper would pick off Dustin through the window. Sean would just see the red laser dot on Dustin's forehead while they ate. No matter how it would happen, Sean could not have been more pleased with himself. He got a message to the outside. His months of caution and patience had paid off.

Soon, he would be free from these lunatics. And he could go back to the real world. Those thoughts eased him into sleep and dreams of home.

. . . . . . .

When Saturday finally came, Sean took a long hot shower, leaning against the shower wall to nurse his bad leg. Ignoring the sting of the heat on the cuts, he wanted to be as clean as possible for when Mason came home that day. Getting away from Dustin would be a blessing itself, and from there, Mason would be completely unsuspecting of what would happen within the days to come. Even with hope in clear sight, Sean imagined how Mason might react to seeing Sean's cuts, welts, and bruises. Surely, he'd be pissed, right? Maybe he would yell at Dustin right then and there. Or maybe, he'd punch Dustin in the face, old movie bar-brawl style. Sean hoped Mason would at least get him some pain meds for his leg. His drugs helped a little with the pain, but his knee was as swollen as it had been a few days ago.

The shower opened some of the cuts, and the water at Sean's feet turned pink. Yet, despite the sting, it felt comforting, relaxing. The steam filled Sean's nose, and he breathed in deeply, conscious again of the collar around his neck, the true source of his imprisonment. He would be glad to get rid of the collar and be back at his apartment, in his own shower, with his own bath towels, his own shampoo even.

He turned the water off, dried himself, and went into the living room. Dustin was sitting on the couch, reading a book. He looked up and looked Sean over with a smile. "You excited to see Mason after all, Sean? Was I that bad?"

Sean shook his head quickly. "No, I just...he punishes me if I'm not super clean all the time."

"Ah," Dustin said, closing his book. It was a book of Robert Frost poetry. "So, what you're saying is that with me you've just been lazy, huh?"

As Dustin stood, Sean raised his hands defensively. "Oh. No, sir! I've just...um..."

Dustin laughed. "It's ok, Sean. I'm nowhere near like your master. And the things I'm into...aren't for everybody." He gave a sly wink as if he had so innocently thought Sean had been *into* being abused and tortured. "Besides, I'm sure Mason has missed his 'Bo' too."

Sean's jaw clenched. "I'm sure he has, too." Sean by no means truly *missed* Mason. He hated Mason only marginally less than he hated Dustin.

"Just be careful," Dustin said, placing a hand on Sean's shoulder. "I would hate for you to be another numbered grave marker in his little cemetery, yeah?"

Sean nodded. "Yeah, I'll keep that in mind."

"What's it been like? Turning into his personal sex toy?" Dustin asked as if it were a point of genuine interest, though not concern.

Looking to the window, half-expecting Mason's truck to appear on the path up the hill, Sean said, "It sucks. I hate it here. I want to go back to my old life. But more than anything, I want to survive." Saying that, he felt a little braver.

"I'd like you to survive, too." Dustin walked over to the door and leaned against it, close to where he had stood the first time Sean had ever seen him. "You're fun. And I think you'll do better than his other 'boys' have done. I can tell he likes you a lot more, too. Stay on his good side, and just do what you're told, and you'll do fine."

Sean wasn't sure whether he should feel lucky or horrified that he had grown on Mason so much. Still, he had knowledge that Dustin didn't: the cops would find him soon. He smiled and replied, "I know I will."

Sean's smile wiped the smile off Dustin's face, a predator surprised by his prey's courage. Dustin snorted and opened his mouth to speak.

Dustin's cell phone rang.

Dustin walked over to it, picked it up, and answered it. Sean stood there, trying to be invisible as he listened intently.

"Hey Mason, how's it going?"

A pause.

"What?"

Another pause. Sean's smile faded.

"Oh, um. Well, that's okay by me. Are you going to—"

Pause.

"Ok, that's great. Yessir. I'll let him know."

Pause. Dustin's smile grew.

"Alright. Have fun, Mason."

Pause.

"Yup. Bye."

Dustin turned the phone's display off and turned back toward Sean, crossing his arms. "Well, I have some bad news for you." He put on a serious face.

"What...what is it?" Sean asked, his mouth suddenly feeling dry.

Dustin grimaced first as he looked at Sean, but then that frown twisted into a smile, full of teeth. "Well, Sean, looks like I'm going to be around another week. Mason had some trouble at the airport, so he'll be stuck there a few more days."

Sean's eyes widened. "No..."

Dustin nodded slowly. "Yes, Sean. Well...since I'm going to be here a few more days...I guess we should get started with today's session...wouldn't you agree?"

Taking a step back, Sean eyed the black bag beside the couch.

"That's right, Sean," Dustin said, noticing Sean's glance. He reached down and unzipped the bag.

As soon as Dustin bent over, Sean raised his bad leg and kicked Dustin in the head hard so that he fell sideways. Sean heard the *thump* as Dustin's forehead collided with the edge of the windowsill. Both of them crumpled, and Sean gasped at the sight of Dustin's blood dripping from the corner of the sill, down the wall, and onto Dustin's face. Sean held onto his knee, begging the pain to stop.

# 10

To Sean's disappointment, Dustin opened his eyes after fifteen minutes. Sitting up, he wiped the blood from his face and rubbed his forehead. "What the hell?" Then, he saw Sean staring wide-eyed back at him, Dustin's cell phone between his hands. "What—what the *fuck* did you do?"

"I—I don't—" Sean started, afraid that Dustin would get up this quickly but powerless to fight back. His leg felt like glass was piercing the skin from all angles, and the drugs rendered him unable to throw a good punch at this point. Yet, despite the agony he felt, he felt a surge of pride, and even his dad was silent. He had messaged Janie more. He would be free soon, no matter what Dustin did to him now.

Dustin grabbed the windowsill and raised himself up so that he stood against the wall. He wiped more blood off his head and spread it against his pants. "Do you know what happens," he breathed, "to boys who fight against their masters?" His jaw hung low, a thread of spit hanging from his chin. "They get punished."

Sean dug his good foot into the carpet and tried to push himself up, too, now fully horrified with what Dustin might do. "I didn't do anything. Really, I swear!"

With a low growl, like a lion in a cage, Dustin lunged forward and swung a clenched fist into the side of Sean's face, knocking him to the ground. Dustin almost fell on top of him but caught his balance. Towering over the collared boy, Dustin looked down at his cellphone on the carpet, noticing that the display was on and bright. He swallowed and shook his head. "What the fuck...you ungrateful bitch."

"My—my *nose*," Sean moaned.

Dustin stepped over the bleeding Sean and bent down to reach for the phone. He pulled it up close to his face and looked at the Messages app that was still bright on the screen. As his eyes flicked over the messages, they widened, and his throat suddenly felt dry as a bone. "You fucking *faggot.*" He aimed a sharp kick at Sean's ribs, to which Sean cried out. "Do you know what you've fucking done?"

Sean did not even bother to shake his head. He knew he was in trouble now.

Dustin started scanning the messages in more detail.

*Janie, its sean.*

*Im at 419 chickasaw rd. a guy named mason kidnapped me and has been keeping me locked up.*

*Hes out of the house now and his fucked up friend dustin is guarding me.*

*Please send cops asap!!!!!*

Then, Dustin saw the response.

*Sean? Is that really you?*

*I'm calling the cops again. They'll be there soon.*

Dustin clenched his jaw.

*Thanks janie. Love you. Please hurry.*

"Janie, huh?" Dustin said with a smirk. "Faggots like you don't have girlfriends. If I find out where she lives, she's gonna be fucked too. Would you like that?"

Sean's eyes widened again, but he still said nothing.

"Answer me, you fucking *cocksucker!*" He kicked Sean's ribs again. And again. And again. Finally, he stopped. Shaking his head, Dustin smiled and bent down to grab Sean's face, squeezing his cheeks inward. Dustin brought Sean's face close to his, so Sean's eyes were inches from Dustin's. "Alright, faggot. You want out of here so badly? Well, consider your wish granted. But I think you'll find that both Mason and I are a lot more gentle than some others." He shoved Sean's head back toward the ground. "We don't have a lot of time, but we'll have to make do."

"M-make do?" Sean stammered. His face was bloody; his side was already bruising where Dustin had kicked him. But his terror kept him more aware than he wanted to be.

"Yes, we will. The plans are going to have to change. If we stay here, I'm going to be arrested, and if I leave you by yourself, Mason's going to hunt me down and skin me himself, assuming he's not arrested. So, I'm going to have to pass you off to Benny." At this point, Dustin crossed back over to his bag and rushed over to the bedroom.

Sean groaned as he rolled over. *What's he doing? What did he mean about Benny?* When Dustin came out with his duffel bag full of clothes and toiletries, Sean realized that Dustin meant they were leaving the house, possibly for good. Dustin threw his bags over his shoulder, walked to the door, and looked at Sean expectantly. "Alright, boy, are you ready? We're going to go for a road trip."

Dustin opened the door, grabbed Sean once again by the hair, and began yanking him toward the stairs, ignoring his screams. Max started barking as Sean bumped down each stair. "Shut up, you fucking mutt," Dustin yelled. This was Sean's first time seeing Dustin so angry. While the man usually kept his emotions to himself, now Dustin was genuinely scared. Judging by the sweat from his head and his arms, he was terrified. His words were all bravado at this point, but his hair was becoming sticky with sweat and blood, and his grip was iron.

"Max!" Sean called, hoping the German shepherd would understand the situation and come to his rescue, but the dog just stood in the entrance of his doghouse and barked. "Help me!"

Dustin stopped dragging Sean and then twisted Sean's hair further in his grip. "If you want, I'll cut you up here and now and leave your bones for the fucking mutt to nibble on. Would you prefer that?"

Sean did not risk shaking his head for fear of ripping his scalp, but he managed, "N-n-no, sir."

"Good, now shut the fuck up." He resumed dragging Sean by the hair, ignoring the moans of pain Sean could not stop himself from making. Finally, they passed the gate, and Dustin opened the trunk of the Camry and threw his bags in there. Then, he moved to the rear doors, opened one, and cleared out some of the clothes that cluttered the floorboards. "Alright, this is where you're gonna lay for a few hours, faggot. So, let's get you comfortable."

Sobbing, Sean was torn between begging Dustin to stop and being completely silent. He wished desperately he had another dose of his drugs though. Dustin held a few lengths of rope from his bag and began tying Sean with them, binding his wrists together and his ankles together. Then, he picked Sean up, threw him into the space between the front and back seats, and pushed him downward so he was stuck in the floorboards, unable to move in any direction. "Be glad I'm not putting you facedown. Couldn't guarantee you wouldn't suffocate." He laughed to himself as he closed the door and got in the driver's seat. The car started up within seconds.

Stuffed into the floorboards of the Camry, Sean could not hold it in anymore and started to cry out in desperation, "Please, Dustin, don't hurt me. Just let me go. Please!" He found a dirty shirt pressed against the side of his face and an empty McDonald's cup against his arm, its sticky residue clinging to his skin. "If I go past the circle, the collar will kill me!"

"Oh, don't worry, Sean," Dustin cooed. "It's not going to kill you."

"W-what?"

Dustin waved his phone between the seats so Sean could see it. "Mason gave me permission to the shock collar controls app. He only wanted me to have it in case the cops came snooping around and I needed to take you outside your usual bounds. He didn't plan for us needing to leave entirely though."

Sean's heart sank in disappointment. If he had known that, he could have disabled the collar himself and gotten out of there himself. Now, he was possibly going someplace worse even than Mason's. "Where are you going to take me?"

"I told you," Dustin said with a smirk, "to Benny's." The car started moving. For the first time in months, Sean was leaving 419 Chickasaw Road, but there was a very good chance that "Benny's" would be worse than the frying pan and the fire. "Now, be quiet, so I can give him a call so he'll know to expect us." Sean heard the boops and beeps of Dustin pressing numbers on the screen.

As the car bumped along the hill, Sean listened carefully to the conversation Dustin was having. His eyes stayed fixated on the ceiling, at one scratch in the ceiling of the car.

"Hey Ben, how are you doing today, bud?"

Sean could barely make out the sound of the other person's voice, husky and Southern, but not the words.

"Oh yeah? That's awesome."

More words.

"Ok yeah, so I got a deal for you. I've been watching Mason's boy this past week—"

Ben spoke again.

"Yeah, but the fucker's done alerted the cops. So, I've gotta get him out of here. And I want my hands clean of him too, so—"

More chatter on the other side.

Dustin laughed. "*Exactly!* How much?"

Ben was silent for a moment before saying a few words.

Dustin whistled. "Considering how dangerous this all is, I'm gonna ask you if you can offer a bit more than—"

Ben interrupted.

Finally, Dustin sighed. "Alright, you're right. One and a half thousand then."

More chatter.

"Yeah, I'll be there tonight with the merchandise. Make sure you have a place cleared up for the kid...mhm...mhm...alright, see you soon, Ben."

He clicked the phone off and then turned his head slightly toward Sean as he drove. "Well, he'll be expecting you soon."

Sean was horrified. He was going to be sold off like a slave to *another* guy. Now, he understood why Dustin had said that maybe Mason and Dustin weren't so bad. He was going to be dropped off into the whole human trafficking circuit. The past few months, he had been a toy, a sex object, a punching bag, and a master's boy. Now, he was just going to be just a lost name, a statistic, and living flesh sold at the value of "one and a half thousand."

Dustin did not wait for a response. He turned up the volume dial and relaxed in his seat. The radio station blared Green Day, and through the tainted windows Sean saw only the darkening sky, trees, and street lights. When it seemed they were drifting into a more urban area, the scenery changed back to sky and trees again, as if Dustin were just trying to disorient him. Sean's legs and arms were beginning to cramp up, and his knee was still alive with pain. To make matters even worse, Sean's vision was getting blurry, and his desire for his drugs was even stronger than his desire to be free from this pain.

For four hours, neither of them said a word, with the exception of Dustin occasionally singing along to the radio. Dustin finally stopped the car. At this point, Sean had no idea where they were, but darkness had started to settle into the sky. He could see stars.

Dustin leaned over the driver's seat to look at Sean. He was grinning. "Alright, Sean, we are here. Now, let me go over a few things with you."

Sean nodded.

"Ben is a bit more...careless with his things. You'll have to do a lot more fending for yourself than you've had to with Mason or me."

"C-careless?"

Dustin smiled and said, "Yeah. One of the last guys he had, he forgot to feed him, and he kinda just starved to death in the garage."

"He starved someone to death?" At this point, after hearing about the atrocities Mason committed on his previous "boys," Sean did not find starvation a particularly gruesome way to die, at least not as malicious.

"Yup. The kid just sat there in a pile of his own shit and piss for days until he passed out in it. When Ben finally looked in, the kid was dead. Of course, Ben still fucked him, wanted to make sure he got all his money's worth before burning the body."

Sean's nose wrinkled. "That's..."—he wanted to say "fucked up"— "gross."

Dustin laughed again. "Yup, that's Ben for you. He's put his boys in dog cages before, made them eat dog food, and if they refused, made them eat shit. He's beat his boys so hard they bled to death. He's gagged them on his pecker so long they died from not being able to breathe." He paused to let that sink in. "As I said...he's careless." He leaned between the seats again. "The best advice I can really give you is this: if you find the chance to get traded again, leap for it." He smiled, showing his teeth, and Sean knew that Dustin was enjoying this immensely. Suddenly, Dustin looked up. "Oh, here he comes." He opened his door, and Sean heard Dustin greet Ben before shutting the door.

There were a few seconds of silence. To his own disgust, he found himself wishing, praying under his breath for Mason to come, to save him from whatever Dustin and Ben had in store for him. He wanted, more than anything at that moment, to be back in his upstairs bedroom, just worrying about having the house clean in time for Mason's return. And he hated himself for that. Then, the passenger door opened, and Sean saw the talkative man who had been at the orgy months before, Mr. Large. He was still wearing a shirt two sizes too small, and his hair looked grayer than it had last time. His beefy hands were poking out of his jeans pockets, and his posture was all confidence, proud to be obtaining a new prize. This clearly wasn't his first time. Sean cowered at the figure, but his ass was already exposed to the man now.

Dustin gestured toward Sean as if he were Vanna White flourishing and showing that there were indeed no vowels here. "Ben, here is your new toy. Boy, this is Ben. You remember him, don't you?"

Sean remembered the way the man had drunk his beer, its foam slopping down his chin, the way he ate, his mouth open to display how his food was processed to mush in his jaws. He even ate carelessly.

Sean wasn't sure what to say. He nodded.

Ben pointed one sausage-thick finger at Sean. "Looks like the toy's afraid of me, Dustin. You'd think he'd be a little more excited to get out of that hermit's old shithole house." His laugh was a roar, as if he had just told the funniest joke ever.

Dustin did not join him "Alright, Ben. He's not your toy until you pay up."

Ben stopped laughing, glared at Dustin, slack-jawed, and grabbed some loose bills from his back pocket. Sean saw even from the floorboards that these were all hundreds. He watched Ben's mouth move silently as he counted the bills to make sure there were fifteen of them. Then, he thrust them into Dustin's hands. "There, you greedy fuckin' prick."

As soon as the money appeared in Dustin's hand, a rusted green Ford Ranger appeared up the street. Its lights were off, but the driver inside was unmistakable. Mason was here, and Sean wasn't sure whether to feel terrified or glad. But when Dustin and Ben saw the Ranger, they both had never looked so scared.

"Shit!" Dustin muttered under his breath.

"He found us. The fucker found us," Ben added.

They both seemed frozen there for a few seconds, as if trying to weigh the possibilities of lying their way out of this predicament. By the time the green Ranger was halfway to them, they realized at the same time that there would be no negotiating here.

"Keep the money!" Ben said, as he started to move back toward the house.

Dustin stopped him by grabbing the collar of his shirt and yanking the larger man back toward him. "You're not going to get out of this scot-free, you fat fuck! The boy's yours now."

"No!" Ben cried. "He's yours! Take him! Let go of me!"

The Ranger stopped at the front of the driveway. Sean could hear that roaring engine slow to a steady growl.

"Fuck!" Dustin said as he pushed Ben back and ran forward toward the house himself.

Sean heard the Ranger's door open and close. He saw Ben struggle to get back up, and then he too was headed toward the house, not once looking back. Sean struggled so that he could lean up and see what was going on.

But he was too slow. Sean saw it through the driver's window. Mason swung once at the back of the man's head, and it split his head right between his jaws, his body collapsing on the gravel, and the top part of his head rolling into the grass. Sean was grateful Ben's head landed face-down. A part of him felt he should be screaming, at least internally, like some blonde chick does in all the movies every time someone dies, but Sean just felt tired. He wanted to be free of restraints, free of pain, and in bed, even if it was the bed at Mason's house.

Then, Mason was there at the passenger's door, his face spotted with blood, and the axe in his hand drenched in the red liquid. His eyes, although ablaze with anger, also shimmered with concern. "Bo, are you alright?" He looked Sean up and down. "What the hell did they do to you?" He set the axe down in the seat and worked the ropes that bound Sean's ankles and wrists. Once the knots were gone, Mason grabbed Sean's arms and helped him out of the floorboards. "Hold still a minute." He looped part of the nylon rope into a noose around Sean's neck and used it as a leash. "C'mon, Bo. Let's find Dustin inside, alright?"

"I-I-I can't walk...sir..." Sean looked at Mason with teary eyes, trying not to break down. He had no love for the bald man before him, but at the same time, even as he felt hatred inside for Mason, his master was his hero this very second. Mason was a monster, but, as much as he hated to acknowledge it, Mason was *his* monster. "Please, sir..."

Mason looked down at Sean's leg and saw the swollen knee. "Shit, Bo...what the *fuck* did they do to you?"

"It was D-D-Dustin, sir..."

Mason nodded and then, without another word, grabbed Sean under the thighs and behind his shoulders and lifted him out of the car. He grabbed the axe and gave it to Sean to hold, too weak to do anything with it. Now outside, Sean saw they were on some hill outside a city. In the distance, a couple miles away, he could see the lights of the city, a small place like his hometown. But there were no neighboring houses between here and there. Even if he could run, there was nowhere to run to, nowhere to hide. So, he let Mason carry him into the trailer with the garage add-on to the side.

They entered through the front door Dustin had left open. At first, Mason walked as if he were going to head to the back of the house, and then they both heard a curse, "*Shit,*" from the door leading into the garage. Mason turned toward it, opened it, and then walked inside. In the center of the floor was a gun case, shells all over the place. It seemed that while Ben was careless, he still took care of his gun. In the far corner was Dustin, crouching down and holding a broom as if it would be strong enough to stand against the vengeful spirit before him.

Once they were in the garage, Mason laid Sean down, tethering the makeshift leash to the railing by the stairs leading back into the house. Even if he hadn't, Sean did not have the energy to run. He was in too much pain, and he craved the drugs to send him into oblivion.

Mason grabbed the axe from Sean's hands and turned back toward Dustin.

"Don't come any closer, Mason," Dustin called. Though his words were confidence and strength, his shaking tone betrayed him. He knew he was going to die.

An axe's primary function has historically been to chop down a tree and separate it into smaller, more portable pieces. A good axe is one that is durable, can last several strokes, and split the wood with precision. And so, it was with that patience and precision that Mason hewed into Dustin. Limb from limb would be an exaggeration. Mason hacked away at Dustin as if he were slicing carrots, carving a turkey, or chopping firewood.

The screams lasted for what felt like a full hour. Sometimes, the screams took the shapes of words. But by the end, they were almost always incoherent sobs. Sean listened to this and watched with a cold distance. None of this felt real. None of this *could* be real. He felt only his own dull and throbbing pain. He almost wished the axe on himself, to stop the feelings, to stop the stinging of the cuts, the shattered pieces of bone in his knee, and the welts on his ribs. He wanted escape. Dustin's finally came.

When Mason approached, he looked like Carrie did in the old movie when blood has drenched her head to foot. The only white Sean saw was in Mason's eyes.

Mason sighed and dropped the axe. "It's time for us to go home, Bo," he said, managing a smile.

Mason threw the parts into the back of the Ranger, even the once talkative Ben and his head. Sean waited in the passenger's seat, and Mason did not ask him to help, to Sean's gratitude. He shook in the seat, and looking in the rearview mirror, he noticed his skin was pale, except for the places it was dotted with Dustin's blood where Mason must have touched him.

Finally, Mason got in the driver's seat, cranked the Ranger up, and they backed out, back onto the street toward Chickasaw Road. Once they left the area, the bloodied trailer no longer in the side mirrors, Mason breathed another sigh of relief and said, "I'm proud of you, Bo. You know that, right?" He placed a hand on Sean's thigh and gripped it, ignoring the scratches. Sean was just glad it wasn't his right leg.

"W-What for, sir?" Sean's voice was soft now. He was not worried about upsetting Mason, but he no longer cared.

"You didn't try to run from me. You did exactly what you were told, and you were a good boy."

Sean thought about his messages to Janie, and he wondered if the cops would be at the house even now, waiting for them, but he did not get his hopes up, not this time. "I thought...Dustin said you were delayed at the airport...that y-y-you would take a few more days."

Mason laughed. "I lied to the bastard." He reached a hand over and stroked Sean's neck. Sean did not react, no longer offended by the touch.

"The house is pretty well-bugged. Wanted to make sure I could keep an eye on my Bo. I heard everything. I was already almost to the house when we were on the phone."

This time, Sean's eyes widened, and he turned to look at Mason. "S-So, you knew about...?"

"About you texting your friend?" Mason asked, his tone sharp all of a sudden.

Sean just nodded.

"Yeah," Mason breathed. "I know. But I've already got that taken care of. Put everything on Dustin. So they're going to be searching for him, and they've got every cop in the surrounding counties looking for Dustin's car. I've already talked to the police on the phone, and they think I'm trying to help them find you. Of course, they're gonna be suspicious, and we'll probably have to keep you in the basement for a while, but not too long."

Sean nodded but did not respond.

"I just...I want you to know I'm proud of you, though. You handled it all very well. But now I'm here...and I'm going to take care of you. You know that right, Bo?"

Sean stayed silent.

"Alright," Mason said and started to unbutton and unzip his shorts, pushing them down to his knees. "Now, use your hand and take care of your master, like a good boy."

Without looking, Sean reached his hand over and started stroking Mason's half-hard dick. His eyes stayed on the road ahead, hoping they ran into another car or a sign or a tree, something to wake him up from this nightmare. And, he didn't want to have to look at that blood-drenched face.

The only stop they made on the way home was past the bridge on Chickasaw Road, so that Mason could dump the flesh from the back of the truck into the stream. "Fish food!" Mason had called back to Sean, laughing at his own joke before getting back into the truck.

Within minutes, the dreaded house came once more into view. In the starlight, the place looked both beautiful and haunted, and Sean wondered if it was the jaws of Hell or the gate to Purgatory he was coming back to. In one second, Sean saw the pain the house embodied, and in the next, he saw eternity staring back at him from those windows. He was not sure which he feared more.

Mason sighed for the third time that night. "Alright, boy." They could hear Max barking in the yard. Through the darkness, Sean could see the blood-covered smile that stretched thinly across Mason's face. "We're home."

# 11

Two months had passed since that haunted night. At first, there were cops who came to investigate the house once a day—during which Sean was hidden behind a secret panel beside the washer in the basement. But now, they came only once a week. They always wanted to confirm no one else was living there and if Mason had heard anything from Dustin. But no, no one was living there—"Do you see any personal belongings or clothes that would fit a college kid?" And no, Mason had heard nothing from Dustin— "But if *you guys* hear something, let me know. That bastard took my good axe."

When the two of them were alone, they never spoke of what had happened with Dustin and Benny. The one time Sean had asked if the police ever asked about Benny, Mason had smiled and responded, "Nah, that's water under the bridge." Sean had grimaced at Mason's sick sense of humor and had returned to doing chores. Some chores became neglected, however, as Sean had a better gauge for what Mason would check for. He didn't bother cleaning out the lint in the old industrial dryer as much. He didn't sweep or vacuum under the furniture. He did the bare necessities, apathetic to it all. He barely spoke anymore about anything, hardly even saying "Yes, sir" to Mason now. Just doing. He poured his concentration into his daily tasks, even trying not to think. Some days, he took extra doses of his numbing drug, and that often kept him in a state of apathy enough to make it through the day. He knew that doing that only made him more addicted to the stuff, but at this point, he didn't have much to lose. His family and friends were gone. Any sense of purpose had been removed. All he was at this point was a human body, still bruised and broken from Dustin's stay.

Most of the cuts had become thin white scars across his chest. But the bruises were still healing. His knee had been the slowest to recover. For weeks, he had to have ice on it most of the time, but now he was able to get up and down the stairs without having to crawl at least. He still could not stay on it for too long, but Mason seemed to have been understanding if all the more strenuous chores took a few extra days. At least, Mason never confronted Sean about it. Sean did his best, without complaint and without care.

Autumn had turned the sweltering heat outside into a nice cool breeze, and the trees lost their own hope, their leaves bleeding red in color and dying. Sean wondered if Janie would be starting graduate school about now. Outside, Sean sat beside Max in the dirt, working on painting the outside of the doghouse. Having had to stay so cooped up the past few weeks, he enjoyed spending as much time as possible outside, and Max, despite Mason's occasional use of him, was good company.

Every now and then, Max would push his nose under Sean's arm while he worked, demanding to be pet. Sean would smile and happily oblige, setting down the paintbrush for a moment to give Max his undivided attention. His black and brown fur was already starting to grow, his winter coat coming in. Sean envied him that covering. Every breeze sent chills up his spine, and the side of the doghouse he was presently painting kept him in full blast of the wind.

After he laid the first coat on the wall, he decided to relax his arm and sit in the doghouse with Max. There was straw inside, and it would keep him out of the wind at any rate. "C'mon, Max," he said as he set the paintbrush down again. The dog, tail wagging, went right inside the house and curled up on the straw. Sean kneeled in the entranced and started scratching Max's head, right between the ears. "Good Max."

He had always wanted a dog. He had just never imagined he would be side-by-side prisoners under a harsh master like this. He heard his father's voice in his head, *"Well, things don't always work out the way you planned them, do they? That's the real world, Sean."* Sean stared hard into the shadows of the doghouse. He was having trouble denying that voice now.

That was when he noticed something in the back corner of the doghouse, something black. He leaned further into the house and tapped Max's back, pushing him to get out of the doghouse. When he groaned, Sean said, "It's okay. It'll just b-be a minute." He reached for the object, wondering what the dog could have possibly found and hidden among the straw.

It was a book of some kind. He held it close to his face, trying to discern what it was by the cover. It was black leather, full of wrinkles, a few scratches, and some dirt stains, too. He held the spine tight and flipped through the pages. The paper inside was lined with blue handwriting. Words jumped out at him as he flipped: "home," "basement," "pain," "dose," "Mason." *Mason? Could this be what I think it is?* He slowed down and noticed that each page held a journal entry, complete with a date penned at the top. He looked past the top of the book at Max and that back corner. There was a pen, too, a blue ink pen.

He poked his head out to make sure Mason was not outside before going back in and opening the book again. He flipped it open to the first page where these words stood out in bold ink: "The Diary of Jeremy Thomas." Sean shook his head. This was crazy. One of Mason's boys left a diary? How had he gotten away with it for so long?

Swallowing nervously, Sean crossed his legs in the straw and started reading the first few entries:

*July 2. So I've learned Mason doesn't ever go in the doghouse for any reason. Probably because a big part of that is my job. I'm going to write in here for as long as I can. Not sure if this is more to me or whoever comes after me. If you're the next boy reading this, I'm Number Seven. I'm also Jeremy. I've been Mason's slave for about a month now, and I hate every second of this place. At least the benzos keep me from ripping my hair out. Or doing something I'd regret.*

*July 9. Mason extended my range a few yards so I can go outside the fence now. Not that it really matters. It's like, "Wow, I can touch the trees now. How lucky am I?" I'm probably just gonna stay stoned at the house anyway. Can I say "stoned" if I'm just on benzos? Fuck if I know.*

*July 20. Had my third gangbang yesterday. Eight guys were there. They're all traffickers I think. Never even knew that sex trafficking was a thing that happened in TN. Like, what the fuck is wrong with people? I thought it just happened in Mexico or China or something. Looks like we're the unlucky ones. We seven. Unlucky number seven.*

*Aug 2. Month number three now. I've stayed in Mason's good graces. Believe me, that's the best thing you can do. I never say a word to him, just do as he asks. He usually rewards that. Got a few more yards added on to my shock collar range yesterday, too. Gonna take Max out for a walk sometime. He's good about coming when you call him. Mason trains him with bloody steaks. Such a cute pup. Such a bastard owner.*

When he heard a low rumble outside, he clapped the book shut. There was a car coming, probably the police again. At the same time, the door to the house slammed. "Boy!" Mason called. Sean jumped and smacked the top of his head into the roof of the doghouse. He cried out but quickly replaced the diary under the straw before crawling out.

"C-Coming, sir!" he called back as he ran to the house, knowing full well that the car was nowhere in sight yet. Based on the level of surveillance Mason had placed on the shock collar, Sean was now fairly confident that Mason had cameras somewhere in the woods along the road leading up to the house to alert him when someone was coming. Of course, Sean would have hid in the house even if—and when—Mason wasn't there. If an officer had found him alone, what could have Sean have done? They couldn't remove the collar without Mason's phone, and if they tried to arrest him when he got home, he could just use his phone to shock Sean to death. It was the perfect hostage situation, and Sean was in no place to take risks. He did not want to die. At least not yet.

Once he was inside, Mason closed the door behind him. "Alright, Bo, let's get you downstairs. They didn't see you, right?"

Sean nodded.

"Good boy." Mason smacked Sean's ass with a smile and said, "March then."

Sean obeyed immediately, going down the stairs without question. Once they reached the bottom, Mason added, "Bo, this might be one of the last times. You won't have to stay there long, I promise, you hear?"

Sean nodded. "Y-Yes, sir." Beside the dryer, he went on and opened the hidden panel in the wall that Mason had shown him. For months, he had never noticed that panel. It just blended in perfectly. He stepped inside the small space and held his knees to his chest.

"Nice and comfy?" Mason asked as he picked up the panel.

Sean nodded again.

"Good." He replaced the panel, closing Sean in the darkness.

Sean heard knocking on the front door above. Then, he heard Mason stomping up the stairs. It was not like the kitchen cabinet Dustin had shoved him in, though: he could only hear a few words here and there of what the two were saying above. It was still cramped, though this time his leg didn't feel like it was broken. Here, he was more scared there would be black widows or rats or something.

He closed his eyes and tried not to think about where he was, sinking inside himself.

*But that diary...* He opened his eyes again, staring hard the back of the panel. *Jeremy, that's Number Seven's name. He said it like he had two separate identities. Maybe we do. I'm both Sean and Number Nine. So much of my thoughts the past few months have been seeing me as the* last *one. It depends on how long I can survive this.* Sean had noted all the ways the other boys had died, and he was fairly confident he could avoid their fates. He had already won more favor from Mason than any of the others, it seemed. Still, Mason had not given him the spatial range of freedom he had given Jeremy. He wanted to read more of that diary and see what had become of Jeremy. Number Seven was the one whose body had disappeared, Mason had said. Maybe the diary would reveal what had happened to Jeremy? There was a chance that Jeremy had found a way out. But still...if he had, why wouldn't he have called the cops on Mason? Something to stop Mason from continuing to do what he did? Sean knew he would try to get Mason arrested if he were ever completely free. Not that he any longer had hope of that happening, but still, if anyone could have stopped this from happening to Sean, it would have been Jeremy, if he had managed to free himself.

Upstairs, Mason and the cop must have still been talking. Sean could still hear words but not what they were. He pressed a palm against the panel, envisioning what would likely happen if he were to push it open, walk upstairs, and say, "I'm here! He's been keeping me locked up for months!" Mason would likely kill the officer on the spot, kill Sean, and move to another city. For Mason to have gone through eight boys already, he seemed like the kind of guy who just didn't get caught.

There was no telling how many people Mason had killed over the years, and he had successfully evaded the law entirely. At least, so it seemed. He had stayed out of prison as long as he had kept boys at the house which seemed like a good ten to twenty year span. *It's because the place is so far out in the country. There's no one around here and nothing that would drive their interest. Just an old redneck handyman with a dog and some horses. And the drive to the house makes it even less worth it. The cops probably think that that text from Dustin's phone was a prank of Dustin's, and that now the guy is hiding from them somewhere.* If Dustin and Benny's bodies were ever found, it would probably be some swimmers at a nearby pond who come across their hands or toes or something.

Finally, he heard Mason come down the stairs. He breathed a sigh of relief as the door opened, and Mason stood there smiling at him. "Told you it wouldn't be too long."

Sean smiled back and crawled out, glad to breathe in the cool air of the basement rather than the stuffy heat of the hidden space. "Thank you, sir."

"He said that would be the last time they would pester us. So that's good." Sean nodded. "The bastard said they found a lead on Dustin a few counties over, and they think he may be behind 'your disappearance.'" He laughed. "They haven't even mentioned Benny. They might not even know that he was ever in contact with us. The idiots." Then, he noticed that Sean was looking at the ground. He grabbed Sean by the shoulder and lowered his face a bit, making Sean meet his gaze. "Look, Bo, I'm sorry I've had to put you in there so often the past few months. I know it's not nice. Doesn't come with AC or hot dogs or nothing, but we do what we have to to survive, isn't that right?"

Sean nodded again, managing a weak smile.

"Good." Mason smiled as he said, "Hey, come on up. I have a surprise for you."

Sean raised a brow and followed, wordless. *What has he got up his sleeve this time?*

At the top of the stairs, Mason said, "Alright, wait here. I'm going to go run and get it. Alright?"

Even as Sean nodded, Mason was rushing over to his bedroom. The last time Mason had given Sean a surprise, it was the dog tag for his collar. He still hated that thing. In receiving a new name, he felt like his old identity was wiped clean. *Just like Jeremy's,* he thought. *Except I actually got a new name, too. Not just a number.* Not to mention, the tag made small metallic sounds against the collar every time he turned his head or walked downstairs.

*So, what could this surprise be? If it were more range on the collar, he wouldn't have to go back to his bedroom...*He heard Mason going through a drawer in the bedroom, but Sean did not approach.

Mason finally came out of the bedroom holding a manila envelope with a red ribbon hastily tied around it. The envelope looked new, no crinkles in it at least, and there was no label or address marked on the front of it. "Here you go," Mason said, handing the envelope to Sean.

"W-What is it, sir?"

Mason shook his head, still beaming. "I can't tell you, boy. You're gonna have to open it to find out!" The man sounded like a father giving his son a perfectly wrapped birthday present, excited to see the son's face as he uncovers the surprise. It made Sean think of his own father with his birthday and Christmas gifts of underwear model calendars and sex videos. *"It's time for you to be a man, and start acting like one!"* his father would say.

"Um...alright," Sean said, taking the envelope between his hands and flipping it over. The package was fairly light, and he wondered what could possibly be in here for him. The metal prongs holding the top of the envelope closed bent easily, and, when he opened it, he saw an edge of white, just some papers.

Sean pulled out the thin stack of pages, each formally typed. At the top of it in a fancy curved font read, "THE LAST WILL AND TESTAMENT OF JOHN MASON." He raised one eyebrow. "Your w-will, sir?"

Mason nodded frantically. "That's right, Bo! Look at page three for me."

Sean did as he was told, flipping over to the third page. There was a small section highlighted here: *Upon my death, I bequeath my house at 419 Chickasaw Rd, all of my personal possessions, my Ford Ranger, and all of my animals to Sean "Bo" Wolfe.* Sean frowned. *Should be not survive my death, the above property shall go to the State.* "You're...putting me in your will? F-For everything?"

"Yup!" Mason said with pride. "That's right. Every single thing. All the boxes in the basement. The house. Max. The horses. It will all be yours. When I die, you can be free! You can even have your own boys if you wanted. Add on to the graveyard even." He said this as if he were the most generous man alive.

Even seeing Mason's look of excited anticipation—his mouth open in an expectant smile and his eyes alight with self-pride—he did not know how to react. "Um…" he started. "I d-d-don't understand, sir. Why did you…?"

"Why what?" Mason interrupted, raising an eyebrow.

"Why did you…think to bequeath all this to me? I just don't u-u-understand."

Mason stepped forward, grabbed both of Sean's shoulders, and gave him one quick shake. "Oh, Bo, don't you see? I told you I love you, and I mean that, more than you could ever know. Last week, I went to the doctor's, and they said I have cancer." He paused, as if for dramatic effect. "I know you're going to be concerned about me, and I know this is a lot to take in, boy. Believe me, I know. But we can make it through this together. In the meantime though, I want you to know that you are the best boy I've ever had. I want you to rest easy at night, knowing that your Mason is going to take care of you. Further down in the will," he said, pointing at the papers, "I even write you in for having all the money in my bank account."

"Um…thank you, s-sir," Sean replied with uncertainty, not looking Mason in the eyes, just staring hard at his name on the paper. "How…terminal is it, sir?"

Mason let go of Sean's arms. "I still have a few years on me yet. But part of staying off the grid means I don't have all that full insurance crap. When it hits me the hardest, I'm just going to die here. And you know what, boy? I'm going to want you to bury me at the head of that graveyard, above all my boys. Then, I can join them all and see them again in Heaven. Alright, Bo?"

Sean frowned but just said, "Y-Y-Yes, sir. I promise."

"Good boy," Mason said, ruffling Sean's hair. Sean stood there dumbfounded while Mason headed into the kitchen. Sean squeezed the papers tightly and moved a few feet to collapse on the stairway to his bedroom. He honestly wasn't sure that he could last a few years himself. In his peripherals, he saw his father. He was laughing.

●   ●   ●   ●   ●   ●   ●

Another month came and went, and cold settled into the woods. Mason had been right. Sean never did see another cop at that house, and never would. The Tennessee winter kept the roads icy and slick, and even Mason did not go into town as much. Given Sean's constant nudity, he could not stand being outside longer than it took to give Max food and water. Though it did not snow, it was unbearable.

This of course made it impossible for Sean to get in the doghouse long enough to read more than a couple entries of Jeremy's diary at a time. Generally, the matter inside was just Jeremy talking about getting more range of freedom from Mason and training Max to do things like sit, lay down, and stay. Around Jeremy's fourth month, he started writing in the journal almost daily. Based on his talk about the benzos, Sean could tell the boy had been getting more and more heavily addicted, almost to the point where Mason couldn't keep him fully stocked.

Sean's own addiction had increased since first starting, but it still didn't seem as bad as Jeremy's had been. Sean now took about three pumps a day, while Jeremy was already up to five by month five. As the winter progressed, Sean realized he had been at Mason's for over half a year himself. In two or three months, he would have been there a whole year.

Mason himself seemed to get worse physically, but Sean wasn't sure if it was the vague cancer or something else. He did not feel the need to ask. He just sat there and watched as the days went by and Mason's eyes became more and more shallow, his cheeks sinking in, and a mustache growing long and haggard on his face.

Once the frost started setting on the ground daily, Mason prepared an additional page to the chores list for Sean. He had left it on the counter one early morning before he headed out to town. Seeing it made Sean feel a bit more comfortable about neglecting other chores, like cleaning out the lint from the rickety dryer in the basement, almost daring it to catch on fire while it rocked and bellowed through a drying cycle.

Sean looked over the new list without concern. Clearly, Mason was a holiday man. He saw things like, "Put up the Xmas tree from downstairs"; "Hang Xmas lights around the roof"; and "Always have a cup of eggnog for me when I get home." He realized that Christmas would never be the same as it had before. No family. No friends. No gifts. Not even a warm fire with hot cocoa. It would also be his first Christmas away from home. *Talk about your sad Christmas story,* he thought to himself bitterly.

He sighed and decided he could start with the Christmas lights for now. Mason had taken out a few boxes of them and laid them beside the front door. Next to them was also a power stapler with some paper instructions on how to use it. It was fairly basic: load some staples from a box into the machine, make sure it's either charged or plugged in, and then fire them where you need. Sean smirked at some of the warnings: "Do not aim stapler at face...Do not try using underwater...Do not drink while operating." Indeed, they all sounded like recipes for disaster. Still, he was surprised Mason had allowed him use of it. Perhaps, by this point, Mason knew Sean wouldn't dare try to use the power stapler against Mason. He could only imagine that kind of rebellion. His thin frame aiming this heavy machine at Mason, missing and hitting Mason's shoulder or something, and then Mason taking the stapler and shooting Sean's eyes out with it. He shivered.

After going outside, he set up a ladder, plugged the stapler into the outside wall with an extension cord, and brought a box of lights up the ladder with him so he could start hanging them up.

He held the stapler up to the roof and pressed the button. The staple fired at rapid speed, making him jump. He had never used one of these before, and he was stunned by its power. He planted another staple in the side of the roof, making sure to leave an inch of the metal sticking out to hang the lights this time.

The staples splintered the wood in a *bang* with each shot, and Sean realized fully the kind of damage this gun could cause. *Maybe it would be easier to just end it all...right here and now.* The thought flashed across his mind in half a second, but it dwelled there as he worked. He envisioned the staple entering his brain, and blackness overtaking him, a stronger sleeping pill than the benzos even. Each time, he shot a staple into the roof, he flinched. When he moved the ladder to continue working, he shivered against the cold. *No, I'm too much a coward,* he protested. Still, each clip of metal started to look shinier and shinier.

# 12

Sitting down at Mason's foot, Sean looked up when he heard his name come from the television. "In ten minutes, we show our feature on missing college student, Sean Wolfe, our sports interview with David Deluise, and—"

"Hey, Bo," Mason said, leaning back on the couch with a contented grin and a beer in one hand. "That's you they're talking about. You're famous, boy."

"I'm...what?" Sean said, looking at the screen in disbelief. "I'm on TV?"

Mason took a sip of his beer before glaring at the TV again. "Yeah. Fucking looks like it. Looks like those fuckers think they will still find you someday. They still want to steal you away. But you wouldn't let them take you even if they did find you, would you, boy? You love it here, don't you?"

Sean nodded and repeated, "Wouldn't let them, no, sir." He knew if there was a chance to get out of this house, a real freedom, he would absolutely take it. *Fuck Mason,* he thought, even as he sighed with resignation.

"Good boy," Mason said with a laugh. "Those fuckers are just trying to take you away from your true happiness. After all," Mason added, ruffling Sean's hair, "your ass was made for fucking. What are you going to do out there in the world? Work at McDonald's for the rest of your life?" He took another huge gulp of beer. "Fuck that." Shaking his head, he wiped a dribble of beer that had trickled down to his chin on the back of his hand.

*I can't believe they're doing a whole program on me. It feels strange. Like, you never think the lost person ever is seeing those "Have you seen this person?" flyers or pictures on milk cartons or a TV special on the missing person. Hell, even I've...well...I've seen those same things and thought,* That person is probably dead already... *Fuck.*

They both sat in wonder as the program started.

Full screen was a photo of Sean. It was a picture of his orientation at

STU. He had really tried to dress "like a college student" that day, wearing a plaid button-up, some dark jeans, and his least dirty sneakers. He had even combed his hair that morning. It looked so odd to him now, seeing himself wearing *clothes*. He looked *happy* in that picture. It was like looking at a stranger. His mom and dad were on either side of him, an arm wrapped around each shoulder. Mom was smiling in the picture; Dad not so much.

A woman's voice spoke as the screen zoomed in on Sean's face. "This is Sean Michael Wolfe, age 19. At the time of this picture, he was entering his freshman year at Southern Tennessee University, a little over four years ago. He went on to become a philosophy major, keep a 3.8 GPA, and be a participating member of the University's Honor Society." *If by participating, they mean my signing up and ignoring their emails,* Sean thought with a scoff. "But early this spring, just as Sean was preparing to graduate with a BA, he disappeared."

Mason laughed at this and slurped on his beer.

The screen changed again, and there was a middle-aged blonde woman sitting in a leather office chair with a textured blue background behind her. "My name is Amy Thatcher, and I'm here tonight to tell you Sean's story."

She proceeded to play a slideshow of images, starting with some of Sean's elementary school photos and working all the way up to a picture of him having coffee with Janie their junior year. The whole time, she talked about his life like this was a biography or a documentary. For Sean, it felt surreal, like Amy Thatcher already believed he was dead. Then, she started to explain what had happened the last day he had been seen, even quoting Janie at one point.

That was when the camera panned out from Amy Thatcher, and his mother came on screen. She was wearing a red jacket, and her brown hair was up in a bun. Her lipstick was several shades darker than her jacket. Her face looked tired. Sean noted the dark circles around her eyes, the way her lips were curved downward, the wrinkles on her face that cracked through her makeup.

"So, we have with us tonight Miss Emily Wolfe. Miss Wolfe, how have you been dealing with all of this tragedy?" Amy asked in as sweet a voice as she could.

*You bitch,* Sean thought. *She just lost her husband this year, and no one knows the fuck where I am either. How do you think she's dealing with it? How does it* look *like she's dealing with it?*

His mother managed a smile and started in a soft voice, "It's been a very hard year for me. But I still have faith Sean's going to come knocking on my door any day now." Sean grimaced as he watched her wringing her hands in her lap.

"We all hope so," Amy Thatcher said, nodding and giving what she must have thought to be a sympathetic face. "Well, how have the police investigations been going thus far? Any leads at all?"

At this point, the camera zoomed in on his mother's face, focusing on how her eyes were watering. She wiped them with one hand before continuing, "Yeah, they've had a few leads here and there. There have been so many prank callers and false leads though. It doesn't—" She started sniffling here. "It doesn't really even—" Her face reddened. "It doesn't even feel like I'm any further than I've started." She buried her face in her hands, and Sean felt his own eyes water at this.

Amy Thatcher leaned forward, scooting her chair a few inches closer, and patted his mother's shoulder. "It'll be alright. I'm sure they'll find something soon." She looked to the camera. "This disappearance has been hard for everyone in south Tennessee these past few months, ladies and gentlemen. And we'll hear what one of his teachers has to say when we return."

The screen went dark as Mason clicked the power button on the TV remote. Sean almost asked for him to turn it back on, but he knew it would be no use. The main part of the program was over. In five to ten minutes, it was "on to sports with David Deluise."

"Well, that was a fucking mess, boy."

Sean glared at Mason then, probably his first rebellious move in months, tears in his eyes.

But Mason wasn't looking at him, just staring at the black screen. "She needs to move on. You're my faggot now. She's had her time with you. If she wants another son, she can go get knocked up somewhere else. Move the fuck on."

Sean gritted his teeth but said nothing. His mother was so *sad*. He felt like it was his fault, like he should have tried harder to escape here. He had always been so bitter that she had let Dad be as abusive to him as he was, that she had decided *not* to act. Yet, all the same, he couldn't stand to see her like that. It tore him up knowing she had probably been crying like that every night for months while he had been surviving here, still eating, drinking, sleeping...living. There were probably tens of people who had probably already told her to let me go and have a funeral...but he was alive.

•     •     •     •     •     •     •

A couple hours later, Sean decided to wait in his room until Mason went to sleep. He wanted to spend some of the night hours reading through Jeremy's journal. He had managed to get it up to his room earlier that day without Mason noticing and had shoved it under the mattress. At this point, Mason trusted Sean fully, and even though Sean had given up on freedom, reading the journal felt like a small comfort, a quiet rebellion.

And tonight was the night he would finish the journal. The last third of the diary had featured much of the same the pages before had: further addiction to the drugs, even more extensions to his shock collar range, and teaching Max to fetch with those steaks Mason always kept in the refrigerator. Still, Sean was anxious to learn what had happened to Jeremy at the end. If it was planned and written in the last pages, then maybe Sean could figure out a way to do the same and get back home, to Janie and Devlin, to his mother. The special on the news had inspired him like nothing else had his entire time here.

The paper crinkled noisily as his fingers turned the pages. He had known there were other "boys" who had stayed at this house. He had seen the numbered boxes downstairs. He had heard Mason's stories. He had seen the shallow graves. All the same, he had not thought of them as *real* until he read Jeremy's thoughts on the page. All at once, Jeremy was real.

The last few pages were all one entry, the last entry.

*December 1. Tomorrow marks six months here. Another month in hell. I can't do this. This isn't me. I'm losing myself day by day, and the fucking drugs keep my sense of reality completely distorted. Everything's gray and fuzzy. I don't even feel when Mason ties me down and fucks me. Last night, he did it, and I fell asleep halfway through. I'm dead inside. If I made it home, I would just spend years in recovery anyway. I can't do this.*

*I won't do this.*

*So, I've decided. I'm going to end all of this. Myself. Mason gave me another extension. I can walk halfway to the creek and bridge now. There's a hole under a hill around that limit. It's pretty big. Could've fit a bear once. Gonna crawl in, cover it. Use a sharp rock I found to cut my wrists and just...fade away.*

*Whoever's reading this, whether it's the cops one day or the next boy, please don't judge me for this. This isn't me. This isn't the kind of thing I do. My parents were good Christians. Fuck, I'm a good Christian. I used to go to church every Sunday. This isn't me. This isn't me. This isn't me.*

*And for whatever the fuck it's worth, if Mason gets arrested, please don't put the dog down or anything. Not for the things Mason's training him to do. Just re-train him or something. He's a sweet dog.*

*Mom and Dad, wherever you are, I'm sorry. I love you. I just can't do this, and I hope you understand.*

The bottom of the page had a few dark circles that must have been tear drops, leaving the last few lines smudged but still legible.

Casually, Sean reached over and grabbed his syringe, eager for another dose of relaxation. His hand shook as he held the plastic tool, and he hated it. He hated the drugs. He hated Mason. He hated himself. Swallowing, he thought, *Well, not much I can do about it now. I need it.* And he plunged the needle into his vein. He closed his eyes and willed the numbness to overcome him faster.

Jeremy was right. The benzos kept the world fuzzy and numb. But that was probably one of the only ways that Sean had been able to deal with it at all. If he had had to experience everything with the acuteness of not being drugged, it would have been unbearable. Even the memories were blurry for him. The past few months rushed through his mind: the first gang rape, Max knotting him, Dustin binding and whipping him, Mason decapitating Benny, hanging some Christmas lights on the roof. Everything just felt like a dream. The more it felt like that, the less it hurt.

He set the syringe down on the bedside table, just a foot wide in diameter, just big enough to hold all the drugs and the syringe. He sighed and leaned his head back into the pillow.

He found himself wondering if maybe Jeremy was right, if maybe suicide *was* the best option. After all, it was a way out of this personal hell. All it would take would be one blast from the power stapler. One shot through the forehead, and he would be free.

*But then Mom would never know…She might go on for the rest of her life hoping for me to come home. I can't do that to her. I have to stay alive.* Then, he thought about Mason's cancer confession. *And besides, Mason said he'll die in a few years. Then, I'll be able to come home immediately. Hell, I'll even have a house and a new car from that.*

Then, he imagined coming home to find out that his mother had committed suicide. He could just envision the headlines, "Grieving Mother Kills Herself After the Loss of Her Husband and Son." He opened his eyes and shook his head. He couldn't just *wait* for Mason to die. He had to find a way to fight this and escape. He just had to.

Still, suicide was a much easier option. It would be so simple with the power stapler, much quicker than how Jeremy had done it. It'd be over before he realized he had pulled the trigger. He could even imagine Devlin back home making a joke about it, "I always told him he'd die getting nailed." He smiled at that, but the thought still concerned him. Sure, it was easy, and, sure, it would be quick. But was it the right thing to do?

He turned to look at the drugs on the table. Was "right" what even mattered here? It would make a great philosophy paper, he decided. At this very moment, what should be his priority: being moral and finding a way out for his mother's sake, taking the easiest route and killing himself, or just simple, selfish survival until Mason dies over time?

Even as he pondered this, his thoughts just kept returning to that one material image, the stapler beside the ladder, the whirring sound it made when it was turned on, the strength and speed with which it shot each staple, and the heat of it in his hand.

"You're too scared, aren't you?" a voice said to his left, on the other side of the bed.

When he turned to look, his dad was no longer a peripheral ghost but a full-bodied image, sitting there on an equally imaginary stool. He was dressed in an AC/DC t-shirt, a Yankees baseball cap, and jeans with holes all the way down them. His hairy arms revealed several tattoos from various horror movies, and his black gaze was like the stare of a shark, cold, bleak, and mechanical.

"W-What do you mean?"

"W-What do you mean, what do you mean?" his father imitated with a laugh. "What's with the fucking stutter? I didn't think I raised a retard on top of a faggot."

Sean glared at him. "You wouldn't understand, dad. These months have been rougher than y-y-you would think. You try being gang raped and not come out a little damaged."

He laughed again. "Me, gang raped? I'm not a faggot, remember?"

Sean shook his head. "You clearly need to look up the word 'rape' in the dictionary."

"Fuck, if I had let those kinds of things happen to me, I'd be considering killing myself too. I wouldn't be a man. I would be a weak pussy. And those kinds of men are beat down by the world anyway. Might as well make their job easier. Like you've been saying, one pop from a stapler." He held a finger and a thumb in the shape of a gun to the side of his head and imitated it firing. "And boom. Done. No more of this bitching and crying, alright?"

Sean shook his head again and whispered, "Shut up, old man." He could hear his father's smirk. "I mean it. This isn't...me."

"What the actual *fuck* does that even mean?"

Looking sharply at his father, Sean growled softly, "For one, you're as bad as he is." He pointed downward. "Saying 'fuck' every two seconds is only so emphatic after a while. For two, I don't identify as a sex slave. I might not have wanted to be the sports fan you wanted me to be, or the lawyer mom wanted me to be, but I didn't want to be this either. So instead of telling me to just throw in the towel, you could help me instead. You always told me 'real men aren't quitters,' so...fucking help me."

His dad leaned back on the stool and crossed his arms. "You've got some nerve talking to me like that."

Sean put a hand over his eyes, rubbing his forehead with his thumb and pointer. "Y'know, dad...I don't have much to lose talking to you any way I want to. You're either a figment of my imagination or a hallucination brought on by the drugs...or both. The worst you can do at this point is verbally abuse me—which is what you've done my whole life, so I'm kinda used to it by now."

"What do you want me to say, Sean? This is your new life now. You can't get out of this by yourself. So what can you do exactly?"

"I don't know! I just…"

His dad leaned against the bed, propping himself up by his elbows. "Look, who do you have responsibilities for right now?"

Sean sighed and thought for a minute. "Me, I guess…and Mom."

"Well, there you go. How do you best do right for you and your mother?"

Sean lowered his hand and turned to look at his dad, but he was gone again. "I keep on surviving."

He closed his eyes again and, for the first time, let go. He knew he could not kill himself like some of the other boys had. And he knew he could not fight back against Mason. For right now, his master was his safety and security. The thought terrified some small part of him, the remnant of what he was before Mason had imprisoned him, the dying fragment of Sean Wolfe.

He fully understood the gravity of what Jeremy had said. He was two people: Number Nine / Bo and Sean. Rather than trying to figure out which one he *truly* was, he needed to figure out how to be both of them. He needed Sean's inner strength but also Bo's patience and obedience. Without either of those parts, he would die one way or another. Keeping a balance was the only way he could focus on survival.

He pushed Jeremy's diary back into his mattress and turned to look at where his father had been. "Um…Dad?" he said softly.

No one responded.

"Thank you."

He got up, turned off the light, and started toward his bed. Then, he decided to stand at the head of the bed and look out the window above. All he could see behind the house were the trees that made up the woods of the area. He briefly wondered how much of those woods Jeremy had explored before he decided it wasn't worth it.

This was Sean's new life, and he had only the two options: life out his life as Mason's boy or die. And he chose life. He chose to survive, regardless of what limits now existed over his life. He refused to be a pile of bones a couple feet underground…or a pile of bones in a bear cave under a hill. He had a mother to get back home to, and he had no intention of letting her down. She just had to stay strong, just as much as he did.

The world outside was getting colder, and Christmas was fast approaching. He wondered if Mason would invite his "friends" over to celebrate.

•   •   •   •   •   •   •

The next afternoon, while Mason was at work, probably about to head home, Sean went outside to hang more lights. It was cold as hell, but the warm power tool in his hands made him feel a lot less helpless. He held the power to kill himself and wielded that without giving in to it. He loved that feeling, and he also enjoyed having a new task. Occasionally, Max would bark at the foot of the ladder, begging attention, and Sean would call down, "Not yet, Max, I'll be d-down in a bit. I can't stay out here l-l-long anyways."

He started punching staples into the roof. This was the last side of the house that needed lights on it. When the circuit was completed, the whole roof would be well-lit with different colors every night, Mason had said. Even though the lights weren't to be accompanied with the usual holiday music or the good cheer, the bright lights were still a small comfort for Sean, and he was in a place now where every small comfort mattered.

His thoughts drifted back to the journal again. He struggled to imagine what that would have been like, having Mason have that kind of doubt and suspicion. In many ways, Sean had been lucky. He had stayed in Mason's "good graces" for the most part except for those first months, and, even with the cops' checking in after the incident with Dustin, Mason had been more than patient.

He had not needed to become much more addicted to the drugs than Mason had started him on. And Sean wondered how much of a difference in reality that made. Being drugged at the moment, even his memories of events before being collared seemed fuzzy. For Jeremy, the drugs themselves had to have been a kind of hell, a form of perpetual unawareness. Even Mason had said that Jeremy had had too many drugs. Maybe that's why he hadn't cared too much to find where Jeremy had gone. There really was no way he could have survived that long without the benzos. Even without the collar, he wouldn't have made it back to civilization by himself without dying. Jeremy probably knew that, too.

Sean had another advantage over Jeremy, though. He had stayed conscious enough to be able to really handle the chores of the house with a little bit of energy and fake enthusiasm convincingly enough for Mason. For that reason, Mason had the utmost *trust* in Sean and held a distorted form of love for his "Bo." Sean hoped that that illusion continued to hold until he was able to either escape or until Mason died.

As he wrapped another length of lights around a staple, he heard a sharp hiss behind him, from the woods. He turned and gripped the ladder tightly. Looking down, he made sure Max was still below and not beyond the fence. Then, he stared back at the trees, trying to figure out where exactly the sound had come from.

"Max, did you hear that?" But the dog was still looking up at him anxiously, begging attention.

The sound repeated, a rustling followed by another sharp sound.

This time, even Max turned to the trees and barked.

"W-Who's there?" Sean called. "S-Sir? Is that you?"

He did not like the idea that Mason must have been spying on him to make sure he had been doing work. Had the illusion been slipping? Had he been acting untrustworthy lately? He turned around on the ladder but did not step down, keeping the hot power stapler on the top of the ladder.

"Sir?"

He stared hard at the trees and a group of tall bushes from which the sounds must have originated. Then, he saw them rustle suddenly, and two people emerged from them, a man and a woman.

The female saw him first. Sean watched her eyes light up as she cried, "Sean? Is that you?"

It was Janie and Devlin.

# 13

Turning his head slightly to make sure Mason was not coming down the road, he worked his way down the ladder, trying not to leap down the rungs in his excitement. He almost stepped on Max's tail as he ran over to the fence, a grin stretching across his face as he looked at his two best friends in awe and gratitude. "Dev! Janie!" he cried, unable to believe they were actually there.

Devlin hopped the fence and hugged Sean tightly, kissing him once on the cheek. Then, Janie leaned over the fence and hugged Sean too. "Oh my god," Sean said. "How did you guys f-f-find me?"

Devlin pushed his thick-framed glasses up his nose and smiled, shaking his head. "That's all Janie's doing. I drove us, but this was all her idea."

"How did you...?" Sean asked.

Janie's face was red now, and she was crying as she smiled. "I just followed the address you texted us on that guy's phone. I knew the cops were wrong when they said they had driven up here and couldn't find any sign of you. I just *knew* it wasn't true." She stepped through the fence and hugged Sean again. "I knew it wasn't true. Oh, Sean, I'm just sorry it took this long."

Devlin put a hand on Sean's shoulder. "Yeah, me, too. She thought the reason the cops didn't find you was because the people keeping you had a warning of some sort. So...we parked at the start of the road and walked the rest of the way."

Now that he was up close to them, Sean noticed that they were both covered in sweat, and Janie's hair even had a few leaves stuck in it. "You guys did it...You actually did it. You stayed off the path and so off Mason's radar!"

"Mason?" Devlin repeated. "Mason419? That's the guy who's keeping you here? The guy you told me about coming to see right before you left?"

Janie turned to Devlin, looking wounded. "You *knew* about this?"

Devlin raised his hands. "No, I just knew the name really. And honestly..." He gave Sean a sideward glance. "He had been getting pretty big into the hookup scene at the time. I didn't really think much of it."

Janie looked back at Sean. "God, Sean, what's happened to you?"

He could tell they were stuck between excitement and horror. He realized that he was stark naked except for the collar around his neck, and for the first time in months, he blushed at his nakedness. "I..." he started as he looked down at the ground. "It's a long story."

"We've got plenty of time," Devlin said.

"No," Sean replied. "Not as much as you think. Mason will be off work soon, and I can't let him find you."

"Sean," Janie said, grabbing both of Sean's hands. "You've got to trust us. What's been happening? You've got to tell us what we're dealing with here."

Sean lowered his head. "Um...this g-guy...Mason...he put this shock collar around my neck that one night, and he drugged me. The shock collar makes it so I can't really go much farther than the fence without getting shocked unconscious. He gave me a chore list for every day. He's had his friends gang rape me. Even his dog fucked me. One of his friends, a guy named Dustin, tried to sell me off to someone else in the sex trafficking market here, but Mason killed them both before it was final. So, I've just been trying to lay low."

Devlin and Janie looked mortified, both of their jaws dropped, and they had both stepped back from Sean. Devlin broke the silence first. "That is fucked up."

"We've *got* to get the cops here, Sean. He can't keep doing this to you," Janie said, her voice shaking.

Sean shook his head and swallowed, feeling his eyes water. "It's not th- that easy, Janie. Every time the cops come, Mason hides me away in a hidden panel in the house, and besides, Mason's phone is the only thing that can shut this collar off. It's electric. Who knows what would happen if someone just tampered with it? The cops have come here too many times to count, and they still don't have a clue that I'm here. Mason is good at covering his tracks. It's just...not possible."

"Sean," Devlin said sternly, stepping forward and embracing him again. He said into his ear, "You can't do this to yourself. We will find a way to get you out of here, with or without the cops. But we are not going to let you stay a fucking slave here. Do you understand me?" He paused. "I feel responsible for what happened to you. I should have had them at least look at the app."

Sean cried. "N-N-No, Dev. It's not your f-fault. You couldn't have s-s-s— *damnit!*" he yelled as he collapsed to his knees at their feet. "I can't s-stop stuttering anymore, and I hate it here so much. I want to be back home with my mom and go back to school with you guys. I miss everything."

Janie squatted down to his level. "Sean, don't beat yourself up over this. Everything will be fine. I promise."

"Yeah," Devlin agreed. "The three of us can take on this Mason guy. Then, we can take his phone, turn off your damned collar, and get you home."

Sean forced himself to stand and took a step back. "I don't know, guys." He saw the same wounded look appear in both of their faces. "What if...what if he hurts one of you? I c-can't risk that."

Janie gave him a concerned look. "What do you mean? We *have* to stop him. I know I'm not strong or anything, but there's three of us and one of him."

Devlin nodded and frowned, noticing that Sean was backing away from them. "Yeah, Sean. I've handled some pretty bad thugs at the clubs. And that was by myself. What are you really worried about?"

In his mind, Sean could only hear Dustin's dying screams and pleas for help, for anyone to help him, for the love of God, anyone. But Mason had just kept hacking away at him, like he was just chopping down a tree in the backyard, nothing out of the ordinary in the slightest. "You guys just d-d-don't understand. He isn't right in the head. He brutally k-kills people. It's not like worrying about him having a g-g-gun. I'm the ninth boy he's kept here. He k-k-killed most of the others."

Janie put a hand to her mouth and looked to Devlin. "But...we can't just *leave* him here...right?"

Devlin shook his head and walked past Sean. "We're going in. Maybe we can jump the fucker when he gets home."

Sean tried to grab Devlin's arm as he moved past but missed. "No!" He chased after Devlin, but he was already opening the front door, Janie close behind Sean.

That was when they heard an engine's roar. Mason was coming down the hill, and he would not be pleased that he had company. "Come on!" Sean urged, waving his hand as he moved toward the house. They stood there, seemingly dumbfounded. "You guys have got to *hide*!"

"Hide?" Devlin said with a sneer. "How much good has hiding done you, Sean?"

He lowered his head, no answer.

"That's what I thought. We have to fight back if we have any hope of getting you out of here," Devlin continued.

Still, Sean shut the door behind them, hoping Mason had not seen them from the top of the hill. Max started barking outside. "Look, it's—" Sean started.

Janie interrupted, "Wow, it's no wonder the cops didn't find anything. This place is immaculate." She was looking around the living room in sheer surprise. "There really is no sign anyone lives here except him, is there?"

Sean shook his head.

Then, Devlin turned to him, his brow furrowing and eyes glaring at Sean. "So, have you been enjoying this? While everyone's been worried about you, flower ceremonies, candlelight search parties, TV interviews, and all, have you just been hanging out here, living it up in the country? Getting sex as much as you want, not having to work?"

Sean's jaw dropped. "N-N-No, it's not l-like that at all. I promise."

Janie interrupted again here. "Dev, he said he had been raped and beaten. Even if he's been alive, that doesn't mean he's having the time of his life. God."

They heard the car pull up beside the fence, but Janie and Devlin kept looking around, bewildered tourists in a strange land, as Sean kept begging them to follow him more quickly. "I know this is all weird, but you have to trust me. P-please, I'm begging you."

Janie and Devlin shared a look, and then Devlin nodded to Sean. "Alright, fine. Where do you want us to hide?"

"Thank you," Sean said, leading them to the stairs leading to the basement. "It's this way."

As they walked down the stairs, Janie noticed the numbered boxes. "What are all those supposed to be?"

Sean swallowed. "The belongings of the other boys, their possessions when Mason found them. I have a box there too. That's where my phone probably is."

Devlin and Janie shared another look, but this time it was one of horror.

Sean walked over to the dryer, opened the panel in the wall beside it, and said, "Here, it'll be tight, but it's the only place Mason won't find you."

"Tight?" Janie said, shaking her head. "There's no way we can both fit in there. Seriously."

"You have to try!" Sean said, gesturing with his arms for them to get inside.

Devlin sighed and crawled in first. He pressed himself against one side of the space and waved for Janie to follow suit. She worked her way in, her back to the other side with her legs and feet squashed against Devlin's.

"Now, *please*, be quiet!" Sean pleaded. He saw Janie's mouth open to protest, but he closed the panel over them, hoping they had the sense to stay quiet until he opened the panel again. "Please..." he muttered again, more to himself than to them.

At the same time he stood, the front door opened above him. Sean's heart was thudding in his chest. He headed toward the stairs, and he met Mason at the top of the stairs. "Hey, Bo," Mason said with a smile. "How was your day? Doing laundry?"

"Oh, it was f-f-f-fine, sir." He swallowed. "And, um...n-no, sir. No laundry. Just heard a noise and thought it might have b-b-been a rat, sir.

"A rat?" Mason repeated with concern on his face. "Can't have that now. Do I need to pick up some traps next time I'm out, boy?"

"N-No, sir. I think it's fine."

"Oh, alright." He looked Sean up and down. "Hey, are you doing okay? You look short of breath, boy."

"Y-Yes, sir. I was just um...playing with M-Max outside."

Slowly, Mason nodded as if he were considering whether to believe Sean or not. Finally, he walked back outside, and Sean sighed with relief. *Good, maybe he doesn't suspect anything. I don't know what I would do if he found Janie or Dev out.* At the thought, he wondered how long they could last. Maybe in the middle of the night, he could sneak them back out, but then what? Just send them on their way and say thanks for the visit? The thought made him smirk. No, they wanted to help him. Maybe if he told them everything, they could take it to the police. But would the police believe them? They had visited the house several times already, and if two college kids came to them saying they found Sean naked with a shock collar in Mason's house, they'd probably just laugh and send Devlin and Janie home.

"Hey Bo," Mason called from outside. "Where are you?"

"I'm…" Sean started quietly, then raised his voice. "I'm in the living room, sir!"

"Get your ass out here."

*He's found us out. He probably found something: a shoe or sock or piece of hair or something. He knows they're here. He's going to kill me. I know it.* Swallowing drily, he did as he was told and stood in the doorway, looking for Mason.

"S-Sir? Where are you?"

"Over here!" Mason said, his tone getting impatient.

Sean walked over of the side of the house where Mason was standing by the ladder. Only he was pointing at something. At first, Sean didn't register what it was. Then, he realized it was the power stapler, still turned on, vibrating softly on the top of the ladder.

Mason barked immediately, "What the hell, Bo? Why were you playing with the dog and doing stuff downstairs while this was running? What if it had fallen off the ladder and just started shooting staples everywhere, huh?"

"I-I-I'm sorry, sir. I just g-got distracted…and it was c-c-cold."

Mason's featured softened. "Bo, I don't want you to freeze to death, so just take more breaks. But it's not good to leave power tools running. You're gonna hurt yourself, and then what would I do? You know I can't take you to a hospital. You can't be doing dangerous shit here. You got that?"

Sean nodded, happy to have a lecture at this point. "Yes, s-sir. I promise I'll do better. I didn't mean to upset you, s-sir."

Mason unplugged the stapler from the wall and turned it off so it wouldn't waste the battery charge. "Alright," Mason said, looking at Sean with a smile. "Let's get inside. Don't want you freezing to death on my watch at least, boy."

"Thank you, sir," Sean responded. He was relieved to follow Mason back into the house, his suspicions abated for the moment. Still, the past ten minutes had been the most conversation the two of them had had in months, and Sean was starting to worry he had come off as too defensive.

Waiting for Mason on the table was a cold glass of eggnog, just as he had instructed Sean to do. The larger man kicked off his boots, unbuttoned his shirts, lay back on the couch, and rested his feet on the coffee table, the cold glass in his hands. "Alright, boy, you wanna turn on the TV for me?"

Sean nodded, trying not to speak as much to stay inconspicuous. He flicked on the TV and started to raise the volume, when he heard a thumping sound from downstairs. He jumped but kept turning up the volume till it was almost deafening.

"Hey, hey! Boy, that's too loud!" Mason shouted over the television.

"S-sorry, sir!" Sean shouted back, quickly turning it back down to a normal sound level.

"Shit, Bo. What the hell's wrong with you?"

Sean looked down at the floor and just shook his head, sitting down in his usual spot beside the couch. If Mason hadn't heard the thump from below, then he had no intention of informing him.

Mason frowned. "You're acting weird, boy. Did you forget to take your medicine this morning?"

Sean shook his head again.

"Hmm..." Mason leaned back, trying to get comfortable as he wondered what was going through Sean's head.

They both tried to focus on the television. It was a football game with two teams Sean didn't recognize. After a little over ten minutes, Sean had completely forgotten that his two friends were downstairs. He was completely immersed in the game he didn't understand. It was not particularly captivating, but it was a successful distraction. And it worked just as well for Mason.

Then, there was another thump from the basement, and Sean was sharply aware again. He tried to act like he hadn't heard it. The problem was that Mason *had*.

"Boy, did you hear that?" Mason hissed, standing.

Sean stood, too, but shook his head. "No, s-s-sir. I didn't hear anything."

Mason ignored him and started walking toward the stairway.

"I-It might have come from outside, sir," Sean tried. "Maybe Max?"

Mason shook his head, not saying a word. Then, he began descending the stairs. Sean could do nothing but follow, praying that nothing would happen from this. Mason looked around the basement, trying to find the source of the sound. His head was craning forward, his shoulders hunched, as he scanned the room.

There was a sneeze.

Mason froze. He turned to look at the panel in the wall. Then, he faced Sean in anger and disbelief, his brow furrowed and his fists clenching and unclenching. "The hell...?" he said under his breath.

Sean just stood there, trying to control his shaking. *He's going to kill them,* he thought. *Then, he's going to kill me. Fuck.* And what could he do at this point? Each slow, deliberate step Mason took toward the panel begged Sean to act, to do something. He looked around but did not know what to do. He could neither fight nor flee. Craving his drugs now more than he had in days, he reached a hand out as if he would grab Mason's arm and stop him, but he held it back. He couldn't bring himself to do it.

Then, Mason had his hands on the panel, and he pressed his head against it, listening. He kneeled that for a full twenty seconds. It felt like minutes for Sean. There was another sneeze from behind the panel, deafening in the silence, and Mason wrenched the panel away. Janie and Devlin tumbled out of the space, and Mason jumped back in angered surprise.

Time froze for that moment. Janie and Devlin were both looking up at the shirtless Mason in his red fury. And Sean looked at his two friends in a mix of fear and pity, knowing this would not end well for them, and he felt powerless to stop it.

"Run!" he found himself shouting. "Run!"

Janie was the first up, quick as a rabbit, and ducked under Mason's reaching arms just barely. His fingers brushed her hair, and then she was to the stairs, running up them as fast as she could. Devlin instead ran *toward*

Mason, ramming into him with his shoulder. Rather than knocking Mason to the ground as such moves always did in the movies, Devlin just bounced off, and Mason aimed a punch at his face. Devlin stepped back to avoid the swing and ran into the wall. Mason lunged to strike again. Devlin moved his head just in time, and Mason slammed his fist into the stone wall. Even as he turned back toward Devlin, Sean saw the blood on the wall where Mason had sliced his knuckles.

Sean thought he had known what Mason's anger was like when he was killing Benny and Dustin. There had been a fire in his eyes, and nothing could have talked him down. But now, Sean was seeing a wholly different man. His muscles rippled, and his veins bulged. His jaw was clenched, and his face was beet-red. The man standing before them was rage incarnate, and Sean was terrified.

Devlin ran for the stairs as Janie had done. He tripped halfway up, and Mason was on him in seconds. He grabbed Devlin by the foot and pulled him down the rest of the stairs back into the basement.

Mason threw Devlin back against the wall, the still dripping bloodstain inches from his left ear, and Devlin cried out in pain. Janie had turned and had seen what had happened over her shoulder. She stopped in the living room and called back, "Dev!"

Sean moved to the stairs but did not move any further. He looked up at her and begged her with his eyes alone to run, and then he turned back to face Mason.

However, Mason had not even noticed Janie and Sean's exchange. He was slamming his fist into Devlin's stomach. Over and over again. Devlin was trying to crumple to the ground, but Mason kept a hand on Devlin's shoulder, keeping him pressed against the wall.

"Stop, you're hurting him!" Janie wailed from the top of the stairs.

But if Mason heard her, he paid her no heed. Somehow, Devlin found the strength to swing a fist toward Mason's face. His knuckles connected high on Mason's cheekbone, and the thick sound of that punch resounded through the room. Mason turned toward Devlin, and Sean was glad he couldn't see Mason's face right then. The fire that must have burned in those eyes would have killed him on the spot.

"You want to fight, faggot?" Mason spat, his voice low yet sharp.

Sean moved forward, unsure what he could do. "S-S-Sir..." he stammered.

"Stay back, Bo. This faggot's about to be punished for trying to steal you away." After a few seconds, he turned back to Sean. "Hey, go grab that box of staples for me."

Sean's eyes widened. "The s-s-staples, sir?"

"You heard me, boy. Hurry up. Do it quickly. Now."

Slowly, Sean forced himself to turn around toward the stairs, his back to Mason as he continued to punch Devlin. Sean walked up the steps, aware of the pained look of horror on Janie's face. But he brushed past her, his eyes distant and heart thudding in his chest. *This isn't happening. This isn't happening.* He kept repeating the thought as he walked through the front door, stepped across the frosted ground outside, and grabbed the box of staples beside the ladder. The box was nearly full as Sean had only gotten to do one and a half walls. *What is he going to do?* He found himself guiltily hoping that Mason did this quickly and didn't let Devlin suffer as Dustin had. *Please God, make it be quick. Please.* The thought disgusted him, but the begging kept cycling through his head.

When he reached the top of the stairs again, Janie grabbed his arm, holding him back. "Don't go down there, Sean. C'mon. We've got to get Devlin out of there. That guy's going to *kill* him!"

Sean shook his head, shaking but resigned. "No, you've got to get out of here. Run while you still can. Try the police again. We can't stop this guy by ourselves. You've got to get the police. *Please.*"

He did not wait for an answer. He walked down the stairs, box of four-inch staples in hand. Halfway down, Mason turned and looked at him. "Ah, good boy. Bring those here." He reached out a hand for the box, and Sean saw Devlin, or what was left of Devlin. His friend was a blood-covered mess. Devlin's face was a dark and bloody pulp, the only white coming from his open eyes. Blood pooled and dribbled out from his half-open mouth, a low groan of pain escaping through his cracked teeth. Sean handed the box to Mason.

"Alright, faggot, you're all soaked from all this blood." He grabbed Devlin's neck and started pulling him toward the laundry machines. "Looks like you need to dry off." Then, after opening the dryer door, he shoved

Devlin in headfirst. Then, he flipped the cardboard lid of the staples box up with a thumb and flung the eighty or ninety sharp staples into the dryer with Devlin. When they hit the sides and bottom of the dryer, they made a high clattering sound, like a cat scratching on a blackboard repeatedly.

"S-Sir!" Sean managed in weak protest.

As Mason tried to close the dryer door, Devlin pushed back, attempting to stop him, but Mason just slammed the door harder, crushing Devlin's hands repeatedly. Dustin had made similar screams when Mason had used the axe on him. But Mason just kept banging the door. Eventually, Devlin must have moved his hands because the door finally clicked shut. Sean could still hear Devlin's screams coming through the dryer though.

"Alright," Mason said as he leaned against the front of the dryer, his elbows pressed into the top. "Let's see what we need here." He started fingering the dials. Sean watched him, but he was paralyzed. He looked in terror as Mason turned the dryer onto its longest cycle at its highest heat setting.

Mason turned back toward Sean and leaned against the dryer, still propping up on his elbows. He smiled and tilted his head back, enjoying the heat coming from the dryer and the screams coming from inside. The dryer shook violently now, and, all of a sudden, Sean regretted not changing out the lint more regularly. Tendrils of smoke began to snake their way out the back of the machine, and blood splattered onto the transparent door between Mason's knees.

Each minute that went by, the screams only got louder, and the smoke grew thicker.

# 14

Sean walked backward up the stairs, keeping his eyes on Mason. The man's eyes stared at the dryer, watching the carnage within with glee. With each careful step, Sean made sure Mason was not about to follow. At the top three steps, Mason disappeared from view, and Sean skipped the last three to the living room.

Janie was in tears in the corner of the living room, right beside the front door. When he came up, she looked at him, red around her eyes. "Dev...is he...he...?"

Sean swallowed and looked at the floor, unsure of what to say. "Um...you sh-should have left by now. It's not s-s-safe for you here."

"Sean, I..." She held her arms tight against her chest, and she kept shaking her head. "We came to get you out of here. I-I'm not leaving without you." She raised her head then but kept sniffling. "I'm not."

"Janie, you c-c-can't stay here. Please." He moved as if to hold her. He wanted to tell her everything would be alright. He wanted to go back to watching romantic comedies on his couch past midnight, eating popcorn and pizza, only worrying about grades and what to wear. But he needed to keep her alive. "You have to go, Janie."

Janie balled her hands into fists. "No, Sean. I told you, I'm not leaving without you. We can make it out of here together, while Mason is...downstairs."

Sean put a hand on his collar to remind her that it wasn't that easy, and the sight made her start sobbing again. "Ok," she said, managing to clear her throat. "I'll go. I'll get the cops."

"Thank you," Sean replied, a lump building in his throat as he opened the door for her.

But even as they moved through the doorway, Mason started up the stairs, his boots thudding against the wood. "Bo!" Mason called. "Stop the girl!"

Sean turned to Janie. "Run! Go!"

But she hesitated. Caught in the moment, she did not know what to do, like a coin spinning slowly on its side, unsure whether to fall on heads or tails or even to fall at all. She bolted but seconds too late.

Mason rushed past Sean, knocking him back against the doorframe so he lost his breath. Janie screamed out when she looked over her shoulder and saw the half-naked behemoth run down the stairs toward her. Max was barking as Mason grabbed her arm and yanked it hard. She fell to the frozen dirt and tried her hardest to pull away.

Sean could only watch the scene from the doorway, mouth agape and heart thudding, but just as frozen as the ground outside.

Janie started clawing at Mason's arms, and Sean watched as the lines became ribbons of blood on his skin. And Sean was amazed. The god *could* bleed after all. His master was a mortal.

Mason punched Janie once in the face, and her head went face down onto the ground. Had she been knocked out? Then, Mason lifted her by the hair, and, though her face was covered in blood and frost, she was screaming. "*Sean! Sean!*" Hearing his name wailed like that was unbearable. He didn't know what to do or what he could do even.

As Mason began dragging Janie by her hair, ignoring her screams, Sean clamped his hands on his ears, trying not to hear. She yelled at the top of her lungs, "Let me *go!*" But Sean knew Mason would do no such thing, not until he was sure she was dead. And Sean just wished it was over, wished that Devlin and Janie had never come here, that he didn't have to see this happen to them.

"Alright, Bo," Mason said with a grunt as he got her to the steps. "What should we do with this one? We could put her in the panel-space and put the dryer in front of it so she couldn't get out?" Janie screamed in protest. "Or maybe we could give her to the horses? Your call, boy." By this point, Mason was grinning. To Sean, it looked like a wolf's smile.

Sean shook his head hard. "N-N-No, sir. Please, no."

Mason's grin vanished. "No? Fine, I'll take care of it myself. Stay out of my way, boy."

Then, he pulled Janie up the stairs, using her hair as a leash of sorts, just yanking on it whenever she was stuck on a step. While she yelled out for him to stop, that it hurt, Sean kept chanting, "Please, no," over and over, half to himself and half to Mason. He followed the two, putting his hands to his face, trying to stop himself from vomiting or screaming or wailing like Janie was. He dragged her down the hall and into the bathroom.

Mason yelled, "Alright, cunt, now we're going to see how much you like bleach up your fucking pussy, aren't we?"

Janie screamed in response, both begging for him to stop and for Sean to help. And he stood in the doorway, watching as Mason pulled a white container from under the sink.

Sean felt something snap within him. It was a tangible and audible break. Maybe it was all the noise, between Janie's screams and Max's barks. Maybe it was the thought of his dad telling him to be a man, any kind of man. Or maybe it was just the primal instinct to fight, to lose oneself to the brutal fires that raged within, the same inferno that consumed Mason. But when that dam broke, nothing could stop the flood that filled him. He charged at Mason while he hovered over the counter, grabbing at his waist. His own energy surprised him, but he kept his momentum going, knocking Mason against the wall so his head cracked against a mirror, splintering it in a spiderweb of cracks.

The larger man let out an "oof!" before Sean stepped back and aimed a punch at Mason's face. Blood sprayed from Mason's nose and splashed against the linoleum tile. Mason groaned and rolled his head to the other side, but his eyes were closed. He was either out cold or he was faking it very well.

"Sean..." Janie said, rising to a kneeling position. "Sean, you got him." They both kept their eyes on Mason, watching his hairy chest rise and fall. His breath sounded labored as if he were breathing through liquid, and he very well might have for the amount of blood that was trickling from his nose.

"Y-Yeah," Sean agreed. "I got him." Whether it was the element of surprise or a rare spur of adrenaline, he had bested Mason all in one hit. "Are y-you alright?"

Janie nodded. "Yeah, I think so." She finally turned to him. "Now, how do we get that collar off?"

Sean shook his head. "J-Janie, I need you to g-g-go get your car."

"What? What if he gets up?"

"I'll handle him. I need to use his phone to g-g-get the collar off, but that won't do us any good if we don't get the car."

Janie held out her hands. "Sean, no. The car is all the way at the start of the road. It took us over an hour to walk that far."

"Um...can you drive stick shift?"

She lowered her hands. "You want me to drive his car?"

He gave her a soft but teary-eyed look.

"Alright, fine. Give me his keys, and I can try to figure it out."

Keeping his eye on Mason's face, he reached down toward his pants and unclipped the key ring from his belt loop. Even when he handed Janie the keys, he never shifted his gaze. "Just honk when you're ready, and I'll be out if I've got the collar off, alright?"

All of a sudden, she wrapped his arms around his waist and rested her head on his shoulder. "I love you, Sean. We'll get you out of here. Be quick, alright."

"Um..." he said, hugging her back, feeling awkward as he did. "Alright. I'll be quick."

Then, she left the bathroom. And he was alone with the beast.

He grabbed Mason's phone, occasionally looking up to make sure Mason was still out. "You s-s-son of a bitch," Sean said, trying out the feel of rebellion on his tongue again. He kicked the side of Mason's leg, not really putting his effort into it, more to show he could do it.

He turned on the phone and saw there was a password screen. In the background was a picture of Sean lying naked on a bed. "Did...did you take a picture of me while I was asleep?" He glared at Mason. "You sick *f-f-fuck*." He turned his attention back to the screen. "Fuck," Sean said. "Alright, let's try some things."

*MASON*. He clicked enter. *Password incorrect*.

*MASON419*. Enter. *Password incorrect*.

*MAX*. Enter. *Password incorrect*.

"Dammit!" Sean yelled. He looked at Mason to make sure he hadn't come around and then frowned. "You've gotta be kidding me."

BO. Enter. *Password correct.*

Sean shook his head. "Asshole." He pulled up the list of apps. They were mostly texting apps, some of them seemed like "private" messaging, as if the texts wouldn't be recorded by anyone, not even where the government could trace them. *That's probably how he stays in contact with the "market." Fuck, those apps should be made illegal.*

Finally, he saw one that had the icon of a black, leather collar wrapped around a smiling dog's neck. *Well, this is it. Here we go.*

He opened the app, HappyCollar, and clenched his jaw at the unintentional irony of the name. He tried to imagine a TV commercial for HappyCollar and saw a small white Pomeranian and its elderly, hunched-over owner looking at the camera, saying something like, "I used to have trouble keeping Skippy from running into the streets. But that was before I found HappyCollar." Sean rolled his eyes. If he got out of here, if they really escaped, he would make a mental note to sue HappyCollar's asses.

*Alright, now how do you operate this thing.* He clicked on MY COLLARS and found one entitled Bo. He clicked the name, and it opened up a set of data: its voltage, its maximum distance, its expected duration, and a few other smaller numbers. He opened Advanced Settings, and that was when he saw it at the very bottom of the list: DEACTIVATE & UNLOCK COLLAR.

"Is it really this easy?" he muttered, checking on Mason again.

He pressed the button, and the lock on the collar clicked open, the whole thing now hanging loose on his neck. He removed the collar with ease, letting it drop to the floor in one rapid clink. The weight was suddenly gone. After reaching a hand up to his neck, he felt that his skin was hard and leathery were he had been electrocuted months before. It had probably not healed right, but it also did not feel infected. Staring down at that collar on the floor, he could not believe that something that looked so small and trivial had kept him chained here in this house for most of the year.

He exhaled, and it felt strange, like he had more room to breathe, and he probably did. He was free. And now, more even than before, he felt like *Sean* again, and less like Number Nine. He had done it. He was the first one of Mason's boys to become free.

He looked down at Mason and shook his head. "What are we g-going to do with you? If we leave you like this and get the cops, you'll be halfway across the s-state by the time they get here."

Then, he had an idea for how to keep Mason there.

He ran back to the living room and up the stairs. Lying beside his bed was the syringe and a few doses of benzos. Heart thudding in his chest, he whisked them off the end table and ran back downstairs. He sat at Mason's side like a nurse attendant and thrust the needle into a bulging vein. "This'll calm you down..." Sean muttered, half-wanting to save some of the dose for himself. But he didn't stop until he had injected all three doses into Mason's arm. Throwing the used syringe to the side, he stood.

He went back outside and picked up the stapler. It had never been turned off. He swallowed nervously as he picked it up and turned it on, feeling it vibrate in his hands. Ever since he had first used it, he had only thought of it as a weapon of suicide. He could never have guessed he would be using it against his master.

As he started to head back to the house, a horn honked, and Sean jumped. He turned and saw the Ford Ranger in front of the main gate. Janie had figured out how to work it. And she was ready to go. He held up one finger to let her know it would be a minute. She raised her palms up as if to say, *What gives?* But he turned and entered the house. He still had unfinished business.

He walked back into the bathroom, and Mason had not moved. If Sean didn't know any better, it looked like Mason was sleeping. If it wasn't for the blood dripping down his face, anyway. Sean bent down to Mason's level, kneeling beside his spread legs and grabbed one of Mason's hands. They were dry and coarse, but the touch did not awake him. Carefully, Sean raised the hand as high as he could against the wall, so it extended a couple feet above his head.

"Here we go," Sean muttered as he raised the stapler level with Mason's open palm.

Click. Bang. Once the first staple shot through one of Mason's hands, connecting it to the wall, the bald man's eyes flung open. "*Ah, fuck!*" he cried. Sean guessed the benzos hadn't kicked in yet. "What the hell did you do to me, Bo?"

Sean did not respond. He grabbed Mason's other hand forcefully and held it up to the level of the other one, and, before Mason could react, fired another staple through that palm.

Mason screamed, a high and even feminine scream, like something out of a horror movie. "The *fuck*, Bo!"

Sean watched as Mason used his fingers to try to grab at the top of the staple, but it was fully embedded in either hand, not even an inch sticking out. Blood was running down both of his wrists and arms. Sean set the stapler down on the sink counter, content that Mason could not go anywhere at this point.

"Bo, help me," Mason said, as if he didn't realize Sean was the one who had nailed him to the wall. "I can't get these staples out by myself. My hands hurt too much for me to be able to force the staples out by pushing, and I can't get my fingers around the metal either. C'mon, boy. Help me out."

But Sean had no intention whatsoever of doing Mason any more favors. The police could now find him and put him in jail for life. Sean imagined himself testifying at court against Mason. Mason would look good in orange, Sean thought with a dreamy sigh. He headed toward the door, ready to leave Mason without another word. At this point, he no longer had to follow Mason's orders. He was still coming to terms with the fact that he was finally free.

Mason's face then contorted into a twisting sob, his skin reddening. *"Why, Bo? Why are you doing these things?"* Every word came out as a half-cry, half-scream. *"I wanted us to be together forever. I gave you a home, dammit! I gave you food and—and water and shelter!"*

Sean widened his eyes. He had never before seen Mason beg like this. Still, he kept his silence, curious to see how Mason responded to being entirely ignored.

"Bo, just—just let me go, and I'll forgive you. I promise. Just let me go. It's really that easy. I have a hammer hidden in my bedroom. I can tell you where that is, and we can get these staples out, alright? You wanna do that?"

Sean did not respond.

Mason pressed his head against the wall and started huffing, "Come *on*, Bo! Don't ignore me like this. How many times have I helped you?" Sean raised an eyebrow. "What about when—when I saved you from Benny? He would have had you dead in a week. Or what about Dustin? Your knee was fucked up good. And I killed him. Just for you. I've always been looking out for you, Bo. When these kids tried to steal you away, I threw one of them in the dryer and burned him alive with a bunch of hot nails to keep the pain fresh. All because I care about you."

Sean took a step backward, away from Mason. Silence.

"*Fuck*, Bo! I love you so much. Don't turn away from me, please! I've loved you ever since I first found you, and I've always wanted what's best for you. Please, Bo, I love you."

"You don't know what love is, you bastard." Sean's tone was flat. He was done caring, and he was done feeling. For the first time in months, he was the one in power, and that power numbed him to whatever emotions Mason claimed he felt. "I'm not your boy, and I'm not your slave."

"But Bo!" Mason started, his voice becoming a high whine.

"No. I'm not even Bo. I'm Sean. Do you hear me? My name is Sean Wolfe, and I'm not your fucktoy anymore. I'm going to have you put in jail, and you'll never, ever hurt anyone else again. Do you understand?"

Mason rolled his head around. "No. No. No. Please, Bo, get me out of this. The staples *hurt*. I don't want to be stuck here. I'm too good for jail. I never meant any harm. I just tried to protect you, Bo. Please."

They heard Janie from outside again at the same time. Sean ran a hand through his hair. He had not felt this excited in longer than he could be remember. *My carriage awaits,* he thought with a grin. He turned back toward the hallway, ready to be rid of Mason finally.

But Mason began cackling. It sounded like a low giggle that filled the house. It was the only sound left in the air, besides the humming of the dryer downstairs. "They're not gonna lock me up."

Sean didn't turn around. "What makes you so sure, you bastard?"

"Because," Mason continued, "I have connections in court. Last time I was called in for a kidnapping case, one of the judges was in the sex traffic market. A little bribe was all it took. He was getting boy pussy for weeks after!" He fell into a cackling fit again, and Sean's heart sunk. Mason managed a few more words between laughs, "And—and you wanna know the best part? Even if I do get put in jail, it'd just be for a few months. I'd be back out." His voice went low and cold again. "And then I'd find you. No matter where you went, boy. The only place my boys ever go is in that graveyard out there. That's it."

*Except Jeremy,* Sean thought as he looked down. *He was brave enough to fight back. Even if it was just killing himself. He didn't die a victim...Still, what if Mason's right? What if he walks away scot-free or just does a little bit of time? What if he comes back for me?* He shook his head. "No," he said aloud. "I won't allow that. You can't do this to me or anyone else ever again."

Mason was still laughing. "What can you possibly do, boy? You can't stop me. You're a good boy. Now, get these staples out, and I won't punish you too hard, alright? Get over here!" His voice warped into a snarl.

*No, I have a better idea.* Sean ran over to the kitchen. He opened the refrigerator door and scanned the contents quickly. "Um..." he started as he looked. Then, his eyes fell over what he was looking for, a Ziploc bag with a few pounds of blood-drenched steak. "There we go," he said, grabbing the bag and not bothering to close the door as he left the kitchen.

He kept walking past the bathroom and toward the front door. Janie had gotten out of the Ranger and was headed his way. He called out to her, "Hey, g-give me a few more minutes. I'm making sure that he's not going anywhere. I just got the collar off."

She called back, "Hurry up! I don't want to stay here longer than we have to."

He nodded and went back inside. He really didn't want her to come inside and see this.

When he entered the bathroom again, he saw that Mason was still crying and begging softly for Sean to stay. Sean just tuned him out. He had work to do and not much more time before Janie got worried and either drove off or came inside looking for him: he had to act quickly.

He started by unbuttoning and unzipping Mason's pants. This earned another cackle from Mason. "Oh, you want to give me a final blowjob before you leave me here?" The benzos were really starting to have an effect on Mason. Sean had never seen him so chill before. "Why, thank you, boy."

"Shut up," Sean said. He took off one of Mason's socks and shoved it in his mouth, hard. He tried to shove it as far back into Mason's mouth as he could so there would be no chance of him spitting it back out. Then, he managed to pull Mason's jeans off his legs, and he swung them away and into a corner. Mason's cock and balls were shriveled and tight against his body.

Sean opened the Ziploc bag and held it at an angle, so that the blood inside leaked out, dripping onto Mason's groin and making a small pool there. Mason started using his legs to kick out at Sean, and one kick actually knocked Sean onto his butt. Groaning, he stood up and grabbed the power stapler again. "Alright, Mason, you a-a-asked for this one." With most of his bodyweight, he held one of Mason's feet down to the tile and pressed the stapler to the top of the foot near the toes. Bang. Mason howled in pain through the sock as his foot was stapled to the floor. Before Mason could recover mentally from the sudden pain, Sean was holding the other foot down and fired another staple into that one.

Now, Mason's legs were spread wide, and he could not move them much at all. Even raising his knees would have caused extreme agony. Sean continued his work. He spread more of the steak blood on Mason's cock and balls and then worked a trail of it upward, up his stomach, to his chest, and then the rest of it on his head. Then, Sean took out the two steaks, crumpling up the bag and stuffing it into a pocket in Mason's discarded pants. He laid one steak right under Mason's balls, wedging it into his ass crack carefully; he kept the other steak in his hand.

That was when Mason's eyes widened in fear and recognition.

"*Max! Here, Max!*" Sean called as loud as he could. Mason tried to wriggle out of his predicament, but he could only move so much, and the steaks stayed where Sean had placed them.

Max came at Sean's call, and the German shepherd had never looked happier. Sean had only known the dog to be inside the house when Mason used him to fuck Sean, but this was Sean's first time really *seeing* Max in the house.

"Alright, Max," Sean said, waving the steak above Max's head. "Can you sit, Max?"

The dog dutifully sat back on his haunches, his eyes focused on the steak and his tongue lolling out the side of his mouth.

"Good Max!" Sean was very cognizant of not accidentally saying *Good boy*. He had gained a new hatred for the phrase. "Now, can you lay down, Max?"

Never losing sight of the steak, Max stretched his front paws forward, so that he rested on all four legs happily.

"Good Max!" Then, Sean started swinging the steak temptingly. "Alright, Max, here you go. Eat up!" He turned and tossed the steak.

Sean's dad had tried to instill in him many values and virtues of manhood. When it came to sexually objectifying women, Sean couldn't do it. When it came to dressing in mostly earth or dark colors, Sean couldn't do it. When it came to liking heavier rock music rather than pop or jazz, Sean couldn't do it. When it came to being able to punt a football, Sean couldn't do it. But baseball was another matter entirely. Just a simple game of catch was probably the one form of bonding Sean had ever had with his old man. He could catch a ball no matter how high it was thrown or, generally, how fast it was lobbed at him. And, in the same vein, he knew how to throw a ball, to aim it, and to see it through. So, it was no wonder to him that from four feet away, he watched the blood-flecked steak make a parabolic arc all the way to land on top of Mason's cock, sandwiching it between the two steaks with a wet, slapping sound.

Max was on the steaks in less than a second. At first, Sean had been worried the dog would recognize its own master and back off. But Jeremy could not have been more right. Max loved steaks more than he had loved anyone. He ripped through both steaks with each bite, and Mason's hot blood only added to the flavor and fed Max's own cravings. The howls through the sock only grew louder—though not quite as loud as the smacking noises of the German shepherd tearing and chewing live and dead flesh alike—and for a good ten minutes, Sean leaned against the doorframe and just watched.

# 15

Sean kept his eyes trained on the mirror, half-expecting Mason to emerge from the front door of the house. But the house stayed still. No doors moved. No faces appeared in the windows. No sounds came from its depths. And no dog came out.

Janie drove, and Sean rested his head against the cold window, his breath misting against the chilled glass. She had asked to use a tarp behind her seat to cover him up, to keep him warm, if not decent. He had immediately refused. He did not want Mason's scent on him. He'd rather the cold. As the truck bumped along the dirt road, he imagined the branches of the bare trees reaching for him, trying to keep the truck from escaping, but they stayed still, unmoving even against the wind he knew buffeted through the woods outside.

He heard the horses whinny at one point, but he did not care if they died of hypothermia at this point. He did look out Janie's window as they started to pass the miniature graveyard. Now, those ghosts could rest finally, and, after they really got out of here, he'd have the cops come and investigate the remains. Maybe, they'd be able to find the families and tell them the haunting news. But when they passed over the hill, Sean shivered, not really from the cold, but as if he felt the breaths of the previous boys against his neck. A whispered *thank you* that seeped into his skin.

Janie slowed down as they reached the bridge, and she inched along it, paranoid of falling into the icy stream. Sean's eyes scanned the water's surface, and, for a moment, he thought he saw Dustin's face looking up from it, or maybe it was just his skull, or maybe it was just a trick of the light. He blinked his eyes fast. He really needed a shot of benzos.

Gradually, the road opened up, and the woods began parting. Then, they turned onto a country road. That was where Janie's clunker of a car waited. As they switched into the car, leaving the Ranger at the end of the road, Sean exhaled. They had escaped. They had made it after all. A car passed by them, and Sean's heart accelerated, frightened it would be Ben or Dustin there to kill him. But the car faded quickly around a bend in the road ahead. Sean sat down in the torn cushioned seat and closed the door carefully, every noise pounding nails into his head.

Once they were on the highway, Janie broke the silence. "Are you ok, Sean?"

The first response that came to mind was, "Yes, sir," but he bit it back. "N-no..." he stammered. "But I will be."

"Oh, Sean..."

He turned to look at her and noticed the tears welling in her eyes, the way they rolled down her flushed cheeks. "Wh-what is it?"

She shook her head. "I don't understand how this happened. How he could do all this to you. To Devlin. We're getting the cops, and...and they'll lock him up. They'll lock the bastard up."

Sean was quiet and thought for a moment. How was he going to explain what had happened? What *could* he say even? Then, he thought of the way Max had devoured that flesh greedily, as if he hadn't been fed in days. *No,* he thought. *There probably won't be anything left but bones.* The thought gave him comfort, a sick sense of relief. He merely said, "Yeah."

The exit signs flew by, and Sean realized they were getting closer to the city limits. Then, he saw they passed the exit for the school.

Janie started again, "You know, there were search parties and stuff for you. They questioned lots of people on campus. People who were in your classes, your teachers...your mom."

"I saw..." Sean said, looking down at his naked feet in the floorboards.

"You did?" she replied.

Sean nodded. "On the TV. I w-w-wanted to get out, but I just couldn't. That shock collar kept me there...for months."

"I'm so sorry, Sean," Janie said, her lip quivering.

In that moment, Sean was almost disgusted by her sorrow. He loved her to death, but, at the same time, he didn't want pity. He didn't want this sorrowful awe stuck on her face. He wanted—needed—to move on. He wanted fanfare and smiles. He wanted Janie to tell him that his mom was doing well and excited for his return. He wanted her to say that he might still be able to graduate. He wanted to pretend like nothing had changed. But his bruised and broken body, his stutter, and his shattered will were all testament that everything had changed.

"Where are we g-g-going?" Sean asked, eager to change the subject.

"To the hospital."

"The h-h-h-hospital?" Sean repeated. "I thought you said we were g-going to the police?"

She shook her head. "Sean, you look terrible. We need to get you looked at first. They'll get the asshole that did this to you. But what good is that if you're not taken care of?"

He shivered despite his best intentions. That borderline parental tone. He half-expected Janie to turn to look at him, and her smile and face would be warped into that of Mason's.

He did not speak again after that, not sure that he believed he was still getting away. He tried to focus on the road, although his eyes occasionally darted toward the side mirror, scanning the road behind for a green Ford Ranger. Janie must have noticed this because after a few minutes she reached out and held his hand. He wanted to pull his hand away at first, now repulsed by the very touch of flesh on his, but he held it. She needed the comfort, and he needed to remember what comfort was.

Finally, they turned onto a main city exit, a blue hospital sign displaying "South Tennessee Regional Hospital" in big, white letters. Sean shifted in his seat. What would they say when they realized he had become addicted to benzos? Would they pity him, and give him another dose? Would they put him through some torturing recovery program? How would the stories paint him? A hero, a survivor, or just a victim? Could he still be a hero if he kept to his benzo addiction?

Even as he pondered these questions, the two-story hospital came into view. She parked the car by the emergency room entrance and grabbed a blanket from the back seat. It was mostly white with a few two-inch square colored patterns checkering down its length. Looked like a baby blanket in design but adult-sized. She handed him the blanket, saying, "Here, wrap up in this. You can't walk in naked."

He nodded, thinking to himself, *Of course.* As soon as the material touched his skin, he remembered what modesty was like. And he felt ashamed. He really was a mess. He pulled the fabric tight around his body and let Janie come around and open the door from him. His body was starting to shake. Even as he felt his inner voice protest that he could get out of the car himself, he let Janie help him out of the car and walk him toward the sliding doors.

Once they entered the lobby of the hospital, Janie left Sean past the sliding doors, covered only in the blanket, and went to the desk herself. He must have been quite the spectacle: all eyes had turned to him. Even the people who looked the sickliest seemed to forget their injuries to look at him.

There were about six people in the lobby, and most of them had their heads bowed, as if waiting solemnly for the doctor to come back to tell them their loved ones had either passed or would have to have a leg amputated. The couple of people who looked like they were waiting for a doctor to see them at all were nursing an arm or a leg, rashes covering it.

He ran through what the doctor would probably say in his mind. He had cracked bones. A benzo addiction that would require therapy. His neck had burn marks. And there's no telling if he got something from unsanitized needles and all the unprotected sex he had the past several months. If he didn't come out of this with HIV or something, he would be lucky indeed, he realized.

Three white-coated staff came out to the lobby after a couple of minutes, pushing a gurney. When he saw they were headed toward him, he tried to shake his head and said, "I-I-I don't need a—"

"Sir," a lady in a white coat said. "We need you to lie down for us. Then, we can take you to the back."

He started to lie down, and as he did so, he stammered, "Um, d-d-do you have any...um...b-benzos?" He saw the look two of the nurses shared, and he winced. He wanted to protest that it wasn't as bad as it sounded, that he wasn't a druggie. But he knew that's not what this was about. They were not here to judge him. They were going to try to help him. He had relinquished his independence for months, and, despite his newfound freedom, he was content with letting them take care of him for now.

As they pushed the gurney backward toward the doors to the side of the receptionist's desk, Janie rushed over and grabbed his hand. "Am I allowed to come with him?" she asked the nurses.

They shook their heads and responded, "No, but we'll call for you when he's ready for visitors or if there are any updates. The police will be here soon to ask you some questions, though." She nodded and squeezed Sean's hand one more time before they pushed him through the doors.

It was not his first time in a hospital. The white walls and fluorescent lights were not unfamiliar, yet, lying on a gurney speeding down the narrow hallway, the lights speeding past his eyes, his consciousness started to design faces in the passing ceiling tiles, no faces he recognized, but faces with grins and frowns alike. He smiled up at them and only stopped when a nurse gave him a look without returning the smile.

Finally, they pushed through another set of doors, and they were in a fairly large operating room. He doubted they would have to perform any serious surgery, but still, if he was as big in the media as Janie had claimed, he was sure he was the hospital's star patient for the day, at least, and probably deserved the best.

They lifted him onto the table, and he started to mumble. "M-M-Make sure he's not f-f-following me."

"Sir?" one of the nurses asked.

"What?" Sean said, feeling his vision get hazy.

"Make sure who's not following you?"

"M-Mason419," he said, looking up at her as if he should know exactly whom he was talking about.

He felt a hand press firmly against his neck, the warmth startling. "His pulse is skyrocketing," a nurse said. "And he's losing color."

Then, another nurse came in through the door, a cool draft pushing in and sending shivers up Sean's spine. "Hey, his friend in the waiting room says she thinks he's on benzodiazepines."

"He's in withdrawal?" The head nurse frowned down at him, but he barely registered her reaction. "Ok," she said, "let's get him on IV for now. Dr. Martin will be in soon."

The idea of a needle in his arm was exciting, but he found his strength sapped already. He could neither beg for it nor protest it. He closed his eyes and focused on just breathing.

Once the IV was hooked to him, he felt his consciousness begin to slip.

He needed his drugs badly. He raised a hand limply, "Hey, I need—I need—"

The door opened again, and another chill blew against him as it closed behind a white-coated man. The gust swept over him, and he fell back into the ice.

•    •    •    •    •    •    •

It was from that white and cold world that he awoke, but it seemed the world had not changed, He wasn't sure what day it was, much less what time. The walls were blindingly white, and his head felt dizzy. He groaned softly, but he was alone. He closed his eyes again and imagined Mason. That was the face he had seen the most the past few months, and it was the one that weighed on his subconscious the most, even now.

With a jolt, he opened his eyes again and tried to focus his eyes on his surroundings. He was now wearing a blue hospital gown. Not seeing his nakedness, he almost thought he had disappeared completely. He looked to the left and saw several clear tubes trailing from the side of the bed to an IV stand, pumping something into him, probably keeping him alive. Further to the left were a series of machines with large displays, various lines and numbers across the monitors.

As crazy as it still seemed, he was alive. Yet, the quiet was suspicious. He wanted to pull the IV tubes out of his arm and run, knowing he could not escape Mason if he was tied down in bed. *No, I'm not tied down,* he thought. Then, he remembered the last time he had seen Mason, a puddle of blood sitting in the three-dimensional shape of a human. He felt the urge to vomit, but, when he raised his head a few inches, waves of pain like shattered glass splintered through his head, and he fell back, groaning.

He drifted again, not into ice this time, but into darkness.

•    •    •    •    •    •    •

A feeling of warmth woke him what felt like mere seconds later. His head didn't hurt as much, so he eased his eyes open. There was now a blanket over him, but otherwise, the view in front of him seemed the same. He noticed suddenly there was pressure on his hand, a pressure that hadn't been there before. In fright, he tilted his head back a few inches, expecting Mason to be there, holding the shock collar toward him. But it was his mother. His mother was there.

"Oh, Sean..." she said, suddenly the softest and most comforting voice he had ever heard.

"Mom," Sean said, his voice scratchy. He tried to clear his throat.

She reached to a table beside her and lifted a cup of water. "Want some water?" she said, a pained expression on her face.

He nodded his head an inch. "Y-Yes, please."

She winced and then brought the cup to his lips, hovering over him. "Janie said you had developed a stutter. I didn't want to believe it."

Now, Sean felt his own face scrunch together, and his lip started to quiver. "I'm s-s-so sorry, Mom. I didn't mean to ups-s-set you."

She ran a soft hand through his hair and whispered, "Shhh..." She pet him like a dog, and, despite what he had been through, he welcomed it.

"I'm just so, so, so s-s-s-sorry," he sputtered, tears starting to roll down his face and snot bubbling in his nose. He felt will just drain from him. He was willing to do anything if he could just not be hurt again. He wanted to forget everything and just fade out. For months, he had fought and fought, and he was so tired of it all. He would take all the blame if needed. He just wanted to be done with it all, and that complete, utter submission that Mason had always craved washed over Sean.

"Sean," his mother said, her voice cracking, "it's ok now. Everything will be ok now. I promise. They're taking care of you, and we'll get you out of here soon. Ok? Everything will be fine."

She reached over to the table again and grabbed some tissues, helping to wipe Sean's eyes and nose and cooing as she did so.

Sean coughed and focused on breathing. "How l-long's it been since I was admitted, Mom?"

She frowned at the question and then said softly, "About a week now."

"A w-week?" he repeated. "I've been out a week?"

She nodded. "Yeah. I've been in every day though."

"What about J-Janie?"

"She's been in a few times, too."

"What about...the guy who...did this to m-me?" He focused on her face, gauging her reaction.

"Well...the police want to talk to you as soon as you're rested...How are you feeling?"

Even as she spoke, his eyes started to close again. Then, he became aware that his father was nowhere to be seen. Somehow, the hallucinations were gone. The pain was still there, and so was the terror. But his father, both the image and the voice, was gone. It was the first time he had thought about the man since he had arrived at the hospital, but as he opened his eyes, it was true. Not even the thought of his father summoned the ghost.

"Like shit," he responded firmly.

She frowned at him but didn't reprimand him.

Then, he stared off toward the door. *Where are you, dad?* He doubted the old man was going to just disappear without some scathing remark or two. But there was only silence. He could not even will the man into existence, and he had no desire to. Had the ghost been real? Just a figment of his drug-addled brain? An imaginary friend to battle the loneliness of living at Mason's? Or something else entirely?

"Wh-What are you thinking about, Sean?" His mother squeezed his hand again.

"Dad," he answered truthfully.

She nodded. "I've been missing you both."

Sean felt himself on the verge of tears, but he held them back, saying, "Well, I-I-I'm here now, Mom."

She smiled. "That's right. You're here now. You're back."

Somewhere in the far reaches of his mind, he heard the deep voice resonate, "*He didn't come back alone though, now, did he?*" Sean shivered. The voice was doubled, a mix of Mason's and his father's.

"Mom," he said, his voice dry and scratchy.

"Yes?"

He swallowed. "Will I be able to finish school still?"

She laughed. "Yeah, Sean. I'm sure they'll arrange something with you. You're kinda a local celebrity right now. And if the school doesn't work something out, they'll have to deal with me."

He nodded and attempted a laugh. "Can I have some more water?"

"Of course," she said, giving him another few sips. "Now, Sean, you need to get some more rest. You're going through some drug withdrawal, but the doctors are working on it. The best thing you can do is rest, alright?"

He nodded again and smiled. "Thanks, Mom."

She returned the smile. "I'll see you soon."

As she left the room, she turned the lights off behind her and closed the door.

He was alone in the darkness. Closing his eyes, he tried to focus on not thinking at all. He wanted to fall back into sleep again and pretend that he was normal for a bit, pretend that nothing had happened, that everything would go back the way it had exactly. But even as his mind did start to drift, he heard that doubled voice cackle in the back of his brain, following him into the shadows.

• • • • • • •

The next time he awoke, the room had changed drastically. A table had been moved into the room, and on it were dozens of flowers—reds, yellows, and blues—and several cards with big, bold letters, like "GET WELL SOON SEAN!" and "WE LOVE YOU!" He frowned. *What is all this for?* he thought as he closed his eyes and swallowed. *Fuck, they need to turn down the lights a bit.*

He looked around, feeling his strength somewhat rejuvenated. On the other side of the bed were other gifts: boxes of different sizes and colors with ribbons and bows decorating them, large stuffed teddy bears, and circular boxes of candy with holiday designs.

*Are these...Christmas presents?* he wondered. *I've never gotten this many.* He was as confused as ever.

But the more he scrutinized the gifts, the more he started to pick up on names he had never known before, at least not in his family: Marcus, Jacob, Wanda, Katie, Rebecca, Juan, Thomas... Granted, he could not see many of the names from his place in the high hospital bed, but, from what he could see, most of these were just not from his family.

He tried to move an arm toward the table on his right. It was easy to move, but his muscles shook a bit, trembling. He grabbed a card at random and pulled it open, close to his face.

This was the one with "GET WELL SOON SEAN!" in big red letters on the front. On the inside, it had a picture of reindeer flying through the night sky and a little note at the bottom. It read, "My name is Lissa, and I'm a fifth-grader at Beauregard Middle School. We are sending our prayers for you, and we hope you get well soon!"

*Mom wasn't kidding...* he thought.

"Sean?" a voice asked from the doorway. It was Janie. She was here. She was alive. "Are you awake?" She pushed her way through the door without waiting for a response.

He smiled at her. "Hey, bitch."

She smiled back. "You are awake!" She walked over and instantly moved to hug him. He faked a groan, not ready for a lot of physical contact still.

"Hey, sorry, still a bit um...sore."

She nodded, understanding but sad. "Sure, no problem. How are you feeling otherwise?"

Sean looked down toward his feet. "Still recovering, I guess. Not really sure how to feel yet." He tried to change the subject. "What's with all the g-gifts? I don't understand."

She beamed again. "Well, let's say you have a lot of admirers. A lot of the local schools, churches, and volunteer places have pitched in to send you gifts and cards, wishing you well."

"B-B-But why?"

"Because," she started, "stuff like this just doesn't happen here. People don't go missing. And—it's like—when you went missing, the whole community got involved. They kinda feel like...like they helped. They feel responsible for you a bit."

Rather than feeling overjoyed at this though, Sean felt enraged. "Like they h-h-h-h-helped? All it would have taken would have b-been for the cops to be somewhat c-c-c-*competent* at their jobs." His frown deepened. "And what about Devlin? Yeah, I went missing, but he f-f-fucking *died*."

Janie looked horrified. "Yeah, but that's not their fault. It's not yours either. That's Mason's."

At the sound of his name, his anger melted instantly. His voice softened. "Did they...did they f-f-find him?" he asked, trying to sound like he had no idea what had happened to John Mason.

She nodded cautiously. "Yeah, Sean...he died."

"How?"

She studied his face to try to garner some kind of motive for his curiosity. "It was the dog. After we left him, the dog um...ate him alive..."

Sean made as much a face of disgust as he could fake. When that proved difficult, he tried to bury his face in the sheets. Janie rushed to sit beside him and rub his shoulder.

"I'm sorry, Sean. I didn't mean to upset you. But...at least now he won't come after you again. It's over. It's really over for you."

His eyes widened. "Wh-What about Max?"

"Who?"

"Max...the dog?'

"Oh," she said, squeezing his hand, "they said they were going to put him down soon. It's not good to have an animal like that running wild. Can't really be offered up for adoption either, you know."

"No, I...loved that dog. I don't want him killed. I..." He remembered something then, Mason's will. "I need to talk to the police."

Janie nodded. "Yeah, they need to talk to you, too." She squeezed his hand again. "You've been out for about two weeks, but, if you're feeling up to it, they're probably going to let you go soon and just have you come in once week or so."

"Okay," Sean responded. He was fine with that.

"Y'know, Sean, a lot of people want to hear your story." This time, when she squeezed his hand, he jerked it away.

"You're hurting me," he said, his face in pain. "I'll talk to the media when I feel like it. Right now, I just want to talk to the police. They have something that belongs to me."

"Okay. I'll be right back." Janie got up to leave and got to the door.

"Janie, wait." She turned to look at him, a wounded look in her eyes. "Thank you...for saving me...and for taking care of me. I'm not good at showing stuff like that right now. I'm sorry."

She brightened. "It's alright. Love you, Sean."

He smiled back but couldn't bring himself to say it back. As the door closed behind her, the voices in his head began a deep chant: *They have something that belongs to me. They have something that belongs to me!*

# 16

*Two Years Later*

Sean was on his way back to Chickasaw Rd. By this time, he knew the way from school to the house without having to think about it. The route was still the same, but he had made changes here and there. He had fixed and expanded the bridge across the stream so it was easier to cross. He had helped the State dig up the old graves and return belongings to the families of the other boys, the "lost boys," as the Tennessee media outlets had called them the first few months when Sean came out with what had happened at Mason's house, as if 419 Chickasaw was Neverland and not Hell. He had sold the barn—just the wood anyway—and its horses, making enough to start going to graduate school for Criminal Justice. The one thing that had stayed fundamentally the same was the house itself, despite his small personal touches. It now had a pantry stocked with instant noodles, a few bookshelves mostly filled with mystery novels, and posters of various animals tacked onto the walls. Yet, other than those changes, the house had kept its two bedrooms, its barren basement, and a full refrigerator...still with a shelf for the bags of bloodied steaks.

Mason had written Sean into his will, not knowing how soon his death would come upon him, but the will was just as legal. When the cops had later looked at the house, while Sean was at the hospital, all they had seen were bloodstains and bones in the bathroom and a dog with a bloody muzzle. When the State tried to put the dog down, Sean had protested and testified in court, claiming that the dog had been a big part of saving him. (Of course, Janie and Devlin had been recognized for much of the same. They had even put a medal on Devlin's grave.) And after all, the dog was rightfully Sean's now that Mason had died.

Max greeted him at the fence, tail wagging and ears perked. The German shepherd had grown happier in the past two years than he had been all the time Sean had known him under Mason's control. And Sean loved him no longer as a partner-in-imprisonment but as an actual companion. He had let the dog become a house dog, sharing the couch, food, and even the bed—in no sexual capacity, of course. Just as the dog hopped around the fence with excitement, Sean smiled as he pulled up alongside the far end of the fence. He wanted to make sure there was plenty of room for their soon-to-arrive guest to park.

He shut the car off and sat there a while, looking at the house. At one time, he had called the house hauntingly serene. Its windows and front door had the visage of a face trying to suck visitors in and never let them out. But now, Sean saw it truly as home. If the house had demons, their ruckus was his lullaby.

News crews had been by the house a few times to do different documentary-like features on "Sean and the Lost Boys." He had answered all their questions, often sparing no gory detail and having many of the reporters and cameramen flinch with discomfort. But still, it was a tale worth sharing. He wanted to fight back against sex trafficking in the South, and bringing it to people's knowledge was a big first step in that direction. Starting grad school for Criminal Justice was another such step. What he called his "freelance work," such as the job he had tonight, was a third and probably more immediately influential step. But thankfully, he hadn't had any media visitors in a little over a year. His official address was where his mom lived. The house on Chickasaw was treated as just additional property Sean owned. Just as he had no media visitors, the cops never came out this way either.

He exited the car with a black bag in hand, slamming the car door as he did so, and Max hopped through the fence and jumped up to lick Sean's face, as if he were expecting Sean to catch him and hold him there. Sean laughed and pushed the German shepherd down. "Get down, you silly mutt. You're starting to get too old to be jumping on me anyway. Hell, you *know* you're too big to be jumping on me."

As he walked inside, he set his bag down past the door. "Did you keep the house well-guarded while I was gone, Maxie?" The dog continued wagging its tail in response. "Good boy." Sean pointed to the couch, and Max ran up on it and sat. "We're going to have company tonight, and we have to make sure the place is nice and tidy. You wanna help?"

Max barked.

"Alright!" Sean replied with a laugh as he walked around, making sure the dirty clothes were picked up off the floor and the Cheetos bags were thrown away. Once the living room was clean enough, he grabbed a black tarp from the back closet and spread it out over the couch. It was a fairly thick tarp, and not the most comfortable for fucking, but it was plenty comfortable for other things.

The last thing he had to do was grab some tools from the basement and hide them behind the far side of the couch, away from the door. The whole time Sean was cleaning and re-arranging the living room to his specifications, Max sat there, ears raised, tail wagging, panting.

Finally, Sean sat down beside his dog and began to relax.

"Now, Maxie, we wait," Sean said, stroking Max's ears and checking his phone. He4Him stayed his favorite phone app. Only now he used it for purposes other than sexual relief. Sometimes, he even posted a Craigslist ad. The text was similar in both cases though. Not seeing any new messages, he looked back at the post: "Boi tr4de tonite. Email for details." It was short and simple, and as he had learned from looking through Mason's phone and web history, that's how things were done in the market.

The phone buzzed, and he had a new message. Sean grinned as he opened it. "U sure about this, boi?"

Sean had convinced this man that he was wanting to be fucked and then traded off. He had to admit to being the same Sean Wolfe that's been on the news, and he had needed to give the man multiple reassurances that this was what he wanted. And just as Sean had expected, the man's cock was more powerful than the man's ability to reason.

"U betcha," was Sean's concise response. That kind of masculine short answer seemed to be a standard in the market. If someone actually wrote in full sentences, that would be cause for concern.

"K. 10 min away."

Sean put the phone down and looked out the window in anticipation, although he knew he was still early. The guy had to have just gotten on Chickasaw Road. Sean stared into the trees, admiring the sunset and how quickly darkness was setting on his new home. There had been a lot of struggles the past two years. He had had to deal with STU and getting his Bachelor's degree. He had sought out dozens of medical professionals to help him overcome his benzo addiction, and he was still struggling there. He never hallucinated his father again, but sometimes—no, *often*—his dad's voice would come out of nowhere, when he least expected it, doubled with Mason's. And Janie only sometimes met with him on campus to enjoy a burger. She had claimed he seemed colder now, more distant. He wasn't sure if it was because of the drugs or the trauma, but either way, this was him now. It was who he was. A fighter.

Then, the car pulled up, a red Dodge Intrepid. "Nice car," Sean said to himself as he watched it park behind his own vehicle. Max started barking as soon as the car door slammed shut. "Alright, Max, you have to go outside through the back door. Doggy door, Maxie." The dog obeyed, having proved the past two years that even old dogs can learn new tricks. Looking back out the window, Sean's heart fluttered as he recognized the person approaching. It had taken a full two years for Sean to find this man, and now more than ever, he would have to play his cards perfectly. One second of doubt, and the whole game was ruined. He quit peeking through the blinds and moved the lights dial down a few notches, dimming the overhead lights in the house. It wasn't pitch-black; a dim amber glow filled the living room, dim enough to hide the objects on the other side of the coach from sight in most places.

*Knock knock.*

Sean hissed in a breath. It was Mr. Slender, from the gangbang almost two years ago. The last one. He had finally found the last one. He walked over to the door, trying to keep calm, and opened it for the thin, hairy-chested man.

"Hey," Mr. Slender said in his soft voice.

"Hey," Sean responded. He closed the door after Mr. Slender entered and began disrobing. When the men were naked, it was always a lot easier. He didn't have to worry about someone finding blood-stained clothes anywhere at least.

Sean stripped too and lay on the couch, elbows propped up on the far armrest. The tarp he had laid across the couch rubbed his skin hard, but he didn't mind. He had learned how not to make a mess, and that's what mattered. He wiggled his hips to tempt Mr. Slender, and the man happily obliged, getting on the couch and positioning his cock to fuck Sean immediately. But as Mr. Slender worked the length of his cock to get it hard, Sean reached down past the armrest to the objects beside the couch. He grabbed the first thing his hand touched: an axe. *Why, hello, old friend,* he thought to himself. He waited until the man had gotten into a rhythm and started to moan with the onset of a quick orgasm, seed spurting into Sean's ass. *Le petit mort,* Sean thought with a grin as he swung the axe up and toward his mounter.

The screams did not last long that night, but sometimes they did. Although this would be the last time the person screaming had a familiar scent to Max, there would be others to scream in the months to come, others who had been dealing in the market. These kinds of men naturally lived solitary lives, away from the suburbs and away from any social interaction. Made it easier to deal. But as far as Sean was concerned, this just made it easier to avoid suspicion when they went missing. To Max, they were all the same. When Sean was done with them, he would throw the leftovers to Max in his doghouse, and Max would have his favorite meal.

It wasn't that Max the German shepherd had inherited Mason's love for wickedness. It was true that they both loved blood. It was true that they both loved their solitary existence out in the woods, free to do what they wished for the most part. And the two had loved each other immensely. Even now, Max curled up next to a skeletal hand with a small hole in the center of a metacarpal. But no, Max was fundamentally different than Mason. He didn't bury the bones he kept.

# About the Author

Jonathan W. Thurston is the editor-in-chief of Lansing-based publishing house, Thurston Howl Publications. His first horror novel was *The Devil has a Black Dog* from Sinister Stoat Press in Texas, but he has also published fantasy novels as well as numerous short stories and poems. When he is not writing or reading, he's teaching ballroom dance, playing piano, drinking coffee, and trying to convince his dog Temerita that, no, indeed she is not a cat.

View other Black Rose Writing titles at www.blackrosewriting.com/books and use promo code **PRINT** to receive a **20% discount** when purchasing.

BLACK ROSE
writing™

CPSIA information can be obtained
at www.ICGtesting.com
Printed in the USA
LVHW02s1935290818
588518LV00003B/467/P